Also by W.J. May

Blood Red Series
Courage Runs Red
The Night Watch

Daughters of Darkness: Victoria's Journey
Victoria

Hidden Secrets Saga
Seventh Mark - Part 1
Seventh Mark - Part 2
Marked By Destiny
Compelled

The Chronicles of Kerrigan
Rae of Hope
Dark Nebula
House of Cards
Royal Tea
Under Fire

The Hidden Secrets Saga
Seventh Mark (part 1 & 2)

The Senseless Series
Radium Halos
Radium Halos - Part 2

Standalone
Shadow of Doubt (Part 1 & 2)
Five Shades of Fantasy

The Chronicles of Kerrigan

Under Fire

Book V

By

Copyright 2015 by W.J. May

Cover design by: Kellie Dennis - Book Cover by Design

The Chronicles of Kerrigan
Book I - *Rae of Hope* is FREE!
Book Trailer: http://www.youtube.com/watch?v=gILAwXxx8MU
Book II - *Dark Nebula*
Book Trailer: http://www.youtube.com/watch?v=Ca24STi_bFM
Book III - *House of Cards*
Book IV - *Royal Tea*
Book V - *Under Fire*
Book VI - *End in Sight*
Coming Fall/Winter 2015

Find W.J. May

Website:
http://www.wanitamay.yolasite.com
Facebook:
https://www.facebook.com/pages/Author-WJ-May-FAN-PAGE/141170442608149
Newsletter:
SIGN UP FOR W.J. May's Newsletter to find out about new releases, updates, cover reveals and even freebies!
http://eepurl.com/97aYf

Under Fire Description:

The highly anticipated fifth book in the Chronicles of Kerrigan.

Now that the secret is out, Rae Kerrigan is determined to find her mother. No amount of convincing from Devon, or the Privy Council, is going to make her believe her mother is not alive. Working with Devon and Luke against the PC's wishes, Rae will stop at nothing to find her.

Torn between friendship and loyalty, Rae must also choose between Luke and Devon. She can't continue to deny, or fool herself, any longer. The heart wants what the heart wants.

When the Privy Council begins to question her motives and scrutinizes her every move, she soon finds herself under fire. Those she trusts become untrustworthy. Those she confides in cannot keep a secret. Those she loves may leave her heartbroken. Will there come a day when she can finally feel free to be herself – no matter the consequences?

UNDER FIRE is book 5 in the Bestselling Series, The Chronicles of Kerrigan.

In most fairytales, the princess has to find true love—choose her prince.
But every now and again, there comes a princess who makes a different sort of choice...

Chapter 1

Screw the boys. I'm doing this for me.

"Rae! I mean—Karen!"

Rae heard footsteps pounding up behind her as she bypassed the rows of ambulances and headed to the curb to find a cab. There was a pub that stayed open all night just about fifteen minutes' drive from where they were having the ball. She'd found it during her recon with Julian. With any luck, she could meet Luke, open the box, and get the first real proof that her mom was alive. All within the hour.

That is...if no one tried to stop her.

"*Karen!*" Devon appeared in front of her, blocking her path. "I can't let you do this. We have a job to finish. And you're hurt." His lovely eyes flickered over her forehead as if he could still see the mark that Charles' tatù had erased.

"Who's Karen?" Charles whispered. He and Molly had caught up with them as well and were standing side by side, looking between her and Devon with wide eyes.

"Karen is Rae's cover name," Molly whispered loudly and impatiently. "Now shush!"

Rae swept a runaway curl off her shoulder and stared Devon down. A part of her almost felt sorry for him—he was clearly thrown. One second he thought they were headed inside for celebratory drinks, the next, he was chasing her across the lawn as she made her great escape.

"I have to do this." She kept her voice soft but firm. "The job'll never be finished for you, Devon. But for me, there are more important things. I have to find my mom."

His lips tightened and she could tell she'd hurt him. However, he didn't move aside, and she refused to relax her position. There was a distinct line between them. One that seemed to be getting deeper every day.

"Your mom?" Molly interjected. "You found something about your mom?"

Charles leaned down to her ear. "I thought Rae's mom was dead..."

Molly tossed her mahogany ponytail in frustration. "Obviously in this case, 'dead' implies a bit of wiggle room, Charlie. Keep up!"

Rae closed her eyes painfully before sneaking a glance at Charles. When, *when* would Molly learn to think before she spoke?

Charles met her gaze with kind eyes and gave Rae a soft smile. "It seems I'm a bit behind the times. I'll leave you three to it." He headed up the lawn towards where faint strains of music were still leaking out from the party. "But I'm glad you're okay...*Karen*." Rae could have sworn she saw him wink. He gestured to her tatù. "Hopefully now you can stay that way."

A warm flush of relief crept up Rae's arms, and she watched as he disappeared, grateful for his discretion. Molly, on the other hand, was a different story. "You know Molls, I think you'd better head back to Heath Hall." She tried hard to temper the sharpness in her words, after all, she'd been the first one to mention her mother. "It's been a long night." Then a plan flashed through her head and she smiled. "Maybe Devon can drive you?"

"Oh no!" Devon's eyes flashed as he crossed his arms over his chest. "You're not getting away that easily. I don't know what Luke told you, but—"

"Why can't you see how much this means to me?" She threw up her arms in exasperation. How could he miss the significance? She was an orphan with a chance at a mother. There could be no greater motivation than that. "This is way more important than any mission. And I'm not asking for your permission, Devon. I'm telling you I'm going."

His face tightened once again and he looked like he was going to reach out to her, but he stopped himself. "And I'm telling you I can't let you do that. Who knows what Luke has up his sleeve? He works for the Xavier Knights, Rae, and you just suffered a major concussion. I can't just let you go gallivanting around London without—"

"Who wants to go gallivanting around London?"

The three of them jumped in alarm as Carter appeared suddenly beside them. Rae had been so worked up over her argument with Devon, she hadn't even heard him approach. Automatically, her body switched to the fennec fox tatù. Best not to be surprised again.

"No one's *gallivanting* anywhere," she said through gritted teeth, glaring at Devon. She had been using Charles' tatù, that's how Carter sneaked up on her. What was Devon's excuse? "I just..." Her voice trailed off as she scrambled to come up with a legitimate excuse. It wasn't like she could just tell Carter that she was meeting with an Xavier Knight to find her long lost mom.

Carter's hands rested on his hips as he looked at her expectantly. Devon, standing beside Carter, shifted his weight back and forth on each foot as Molly, right beside him, flitted anxiously in the background.

"You just...?" Carter shook his head blankly, not understanding her restlessness. "Your job here isn't finished Rae. Our future queen was attacked tonight; she could very well still be in danger. You and Devon and Molly are to report back to Heath Hall and await further instructions."

Rae took a breath and tried to steady her jumping nerves. *I have the key, damn it! I have to go!*

"Sarah's going straight to the hospital where she's going to be surrounded by armed guards and undercover PCs until morning," she said calmly. "I'd like to go to London tonight, I'll be back by breakfast and ready for duty."

Carter frowned. "Why? What's going on?"

The beat of silence that followed seemed to stretch on into an eternity. Rae tried to think of something—anything to say, but one phrase kept repeating in her mind.

I have the key! I have the key!

"She's a little shaken up, sir." To Rae's great surprise, it was Molly, not Devon, who came forward and put her arm around her shoulder. "She wanted to get a little fresh air and clear her head before going back to work tomorrow. She did get attacked tonight," she finished pointedly.

God bless my chatty little friend. There were times when there was no one I'd like better in my corner.

"There's plenty of fresh air at Heath Hall," Carter replied. "You're staying in tonight, Miss Kerrigan. You're not going anywhere." He turned authoritatively to Devon. "Wardell, drive the girls back to base, make sure they're well rested for the morning."

"Will do, sir," Devon replied automatically. His cheeks flushed as he avoided Rae's gaze. As Carter headed back off into the night, he pawed the dirt nervously with his foot, a habit he'd picked up from Rae herself. "Well, I guess we should pack it in..."

Rae's blood boiled and she shot him a monstrous look. If it hadn't been for his interference, she could be halfway to the pub by now. Halfway to meeting Luke and getting the answers she so badly needed.

Luke had quite possibly lost his job trying to help her. Devon had literally stood in the way.

"You two go on ahead," her voice was dangerously soft, "I'm taking a cab."

All the color seemed to drain from Devon's face as his eyes flitted to the road. "I'm not sure if..." He fell silent, letting the unsaid implication hang in the air between them.

All at once it clicked and Rae brought herself up to her full height. "For Pete's sake, Devon! Are you afraid I'll just hightail it to London?! Relax, I won't. Because of a certain someone, Carter came and ruined all my plans. Destroyed my chance to find out what happened to my mom. Not that I'd expect you to understand, or even to care." Her own face paled with rage and she bit her lip to calm down. "I'm taking a cab because I can't stand to look at you for a second longer."

With that, she stormed off across the lawn, her gorgeous dress barely skimming the tips of the grass as she used Devon's tatù to make a graceful, if furious, escape. She was acutely aware that she was leaving the two of them—two of her best friends—standing in the grass behind her, but at the moment, she couldn't bring herself to care.

There were bigger things in her life than the Privy Council. Why couldn't Devon understand that? Molly understood it, Julian would if he was here, even Charles seemed to give her a free pass based on the only scrap of information he had. But Devon...?

She was his heart. His whole heart.

The words played back in her head as she ripped open the door to a waiting taxi.

If he couldn't support her in this—this most basic, fundamental thing—what did those words even mean...?

Rae beat Molly and Devon back to Heath Hall, her taxi racing down the narrow streets before the valets could even pull Devon's car out of parking. The second the cabbie slowed, her feet hit the pavement and she flew up the front steps, slipping automatically into Jennifer's tatù instead of Devon's. She suddenly felt she wanted to have as little to do with Devon as possible.

Never before had she found herself in such a rage.

Not even when she found out what Guilder really was—what she really was. Not when she found out that Lanford had betrayed her. Not even when the Privy Council released her homicidal half-brother to terrorize her and the rest of the world.

From the second she set foot on English soil, everyone in her life had lied to her—or at least—denied her crucial information. Her past, her present, now even her future seemed to be hanging precariously on little strings. Someone else was always hovering up above, censoring the things she knew, doling out vital tidbits as they saw fit.

This was her life! She deserved to know what was going on! She wanted answers. Hell, she deserved them!

And now that she had finally gone out and found them on her own, she stood trapped just fifteen minutes away, unable to reach them. A key without a lock. And who had stopped her...?

The room tinted red as she waited, almost with eager anticipation, for the fight that was soon to come. She had changed out of her ball gown, but had found herself stymied by the complicated lace straps of the slip underneath. In the end, she had settled for a compromise, slipping black leggings under the silky, ebony dress. It didn't matter if the slit was halfway up her thigh as long as there was something beneath. Her hair lay in a similar state of dismantle. Half the curls were up, piled gracefully atop her head, while the half she was able to rip free of their million bobby pins cascaded down her bare shoulders, giving her a beautiful, if a bit manic, appearance.

After what seemed like forever, the door clicked and she heard Devon come inside. He was alone, thank goodness. With her superior hearing, she heard Molly tiptoeing to her room upstairs, probably trying her best to eavesdrop on the imminent explosion.

Rae waited with her hands on her hips, leaning against one of the posts on her canopy bed, fidgeting impatiently in her lacy slip. She heard Devon pace for a moment in the living room, then stop, as if waiting to see what she would do. Or maybe he didn't even know she had returned already.

Finally, her fragile temper snapped. "So how about it Devon? Are you going to come in here and face me or what?"

Without so much as a sound, he appeared in the doorway. His bowtie had been clawed nervously to the side and the top few buttons on his dress shirt had been torn open as well. His hair hung similarly disheveled, as if he had run his hands through it many times.

His eyes grew wide when he saw Rae waiting for him. They traveled up and down her body, unable to restrain themselves, from her hair down to the tips of her toes, before coming to rest on her eyes. Her very, very angry eyes.

Then he opened his mouth and said the last thing in the world Rae expected to hear.

"I love you."

All the anger drained out of Rae at once, leaving her feeling rather deflated. Her heart stuttered in shock and her lips parted as she stared at him in the golden glow of the lamps. *He...what?* "You, what?" She had intended to repeat the phrase but found herself unable to say the words.

Devon's face paled. His pupils had grown wide, but despite his obvious panic, he seemed unable to tear them away from her. "I love you," he said again, the words pouring out of him in a soft, rapid clip. "I didn't want you to go to London because you got a concussion tonight and I was worried...because I love you. I didn't want you to meet with Luke because I don't trust him and...because I love you." In a swish of air, he strode across the room, standing right in front of her, baring his soul. "And I couldn't take my eyes off you tonight...because I love you." He squared his shoulders and took a deep breath. "I love you, Rae," he said simply. "I always have. I always will."

Chapter 2

"Rae?! Come back to me, Rae! Wake up!"

Wake up? Rae felt the plush carpet beneath her, but she was lying on warm legs. Careful fingers stroked her hair out of her face as she struggled to comply with the simple request. With what seemed like an extraordinary amount of effort, she opened her eyes and gazed up into Devon's frenzied face. It was as if she lay staring through a long tunnel. She blinked several times, and after a moment, the edges around his face began to sharpen and her vision began to clear. "That was weird," she croaked.

With a bark of nervous laughter, Devon shook his head and tightened his arms around her. "I tell you I love you...and you black out," he muttered, shaking his head and trying to pull himself together.

Her eyebrows stitched together in a confused, impotent sort of rage. "Well, maybe next time you'd like to wear the corset," she said defensively, pulling weakly on the complicated straps. "It's almost impossible to breathe."

His face softened into a radiant smile, his famous dimples shining through. "Here," he said, his hands rested atop hers, "let me help you." He worked in silence for a while, trying to make sense of the intricate design, before he finally shook his head with a slight frown. "It's a labyrinth. I think we need MacGyver."

"Just rip it," Rae gasped. She hadn't realized how lightheaded she'd become. She had chalked it all up to the excitement of the evening and her rapid, shallow breathing.

Devon hesitated, his warm fingers hovering near her neck. "Are you sure? Won't Molly be upset?"

Rae waved her hand dismissively. "She can order me another one. One that won't kill me," she added under her breath.

After an almost imperceptible pause, Devon wrapped his fingers around the lace and tore it gently apart. The straps were no match for his strength, tatù or not, and quickly fell in tattered ribbons down her sides. Without anything to hold it up, the slip also began sliding off her body, but both she and Devon caught it with quick hands. Their eyes met in the middle.

"You love me?" Rae whispered. It was too good to be true. Too simple an explanation to make sense.

Devon's breath hitched in his chest, but he laced his fingers gently into hers, their closed hands resting on her pounding heart.

"With everything in me," he answered, "I love you."

Rae had no idea how long they sat there on the floor, gazing into each other's eyes, but after a while, Devon's face tightened and his hand twitched.

"Rae...a bit too tight."

"What?" She looked down at their joined hands and quickly loosened her fingers. "Oh—sorry!" She rubbed his hand gently with her thumb and watched as the bluish tint slowly faded away.

"That's okay," he chuckled, lowering his head and coaxing her eyes back to his. "You know what Rae...you really know how to leave a guy hanging."

Rae's cheeks flushed crimson as she ducked her head again and pushed stray curls from her face. Devon loved her. What was she supposed to do with that? It's not like they could be together. Everyone from the head of the Privy Council down to Devon's own father would absolutely forbid it. And while he loved her...it seemed like there were things he loved just as much, if not more.

Devon lived for honor and duty. He lived for the mission. Just now outside, he'd stood between her and the possibility of finding her mother just for the sake of the Privy Council.

What did his love mean? If it could be derailed by all that?

"I love you too, Devon." The answer came easily to Rae, after all, it was true. She just didn't know what kind of weight that carried. "I always have—you know that. But..."

He squeezed her hand. "But what, Kerrigan?"

For a moment, it was so simple. Devon loved her. She loved Devon. But then reality sent them both crashing back to earth. "But you broke up with me." It was impossible to keep all the hurt and bitterness from her voice, and her eyes stung with unwelcome tears she refused to let fall. "If you love me so much...how could you do that? I would never have left you—not for anything."

"I didn't leave you, Rae," Devon answered quickly. "I was always there watching, looking out for danger, protecting—"

"From a distance," she cut him off abruptly. "And I didn't ask you to do that, Devon. I wanted *you*, not your protection. If you haven't noticed, I'm quite capable of protecting myself."

"Rae, you don't understand. To have the person you love threatened—I mean, there were people out there set on killing you. I couldn't just...I had to take a step back. I had to let you figure out who you were as a person, fully come into your power. It seemed, well, prudent."

Rae raised her eyebrows. "Prudent?" She had pulled off his lap by now and was sitting beside him, both of them leaning back against the bed. "Do you hear yourself right now? You're saying you're in love with me, I'm saying I'm in love with you. But...you want to do what's *prudent*."

His cheeks flushed. "Okay, dumb choice of word. I'm just saying, you're the most important thing in the world to me. I felt like it was my responsibility to keep you safe."

"So you took the choice away from me," Rae answered quietly. "Imagine if the roles were reversed. If I decided that you needed time without me for your own good. How would that make you feel?"

There was a second's pause before he hung his head. "It would make me feel betrayed."

Rae punched him suddenly in the shoulder and he looked up in shock. "And a little pissed off too, right?"

His shock morphed into a smile and he laughed, flashing his dimple and scooting closer to her on the floor. She smiled back, and when he opened his arms, she slid into them willingly.

"I'm sorry," he breathed into her hair. "I was trying to do what's best, but I was an idiot. You just...you overwhelm me sometimes. It's like I lose my head. Julian's always telling me I'm an idiot."

"He's right." She grinned into his chest, unable to believe the conversation they were having. Unable to process the words she had waited so very long to hear. But at the same time, she had a nagging suspicion that things wouldn't be as easy the second time around. The stakes were as high as ever and it was getting harder and harder to know who to trust. She had trusted Devon once, trusted him more than anyone else in the world. And...he had left her. Could they ever really go back? Could it ever be the same?

But then he kissed her...and nothing else seemed to matter.

It started out tentative. Re-exploring familiar territory, slowly re-opening a door that had been long closed. Then her hands slid up into his hair and everything else became a blur.

He shifted beneath her, and the next thing she knew, she was back in his lap—straddling him as her arms wrapped around his neck. The kiss deepened and became frantic. His hands were everywhere. In her hair, down her back, fiddling tentatively with the straps that had fallen down her sides. She pressed herself up against him to keep her slip from sliding down, but in her haste to do so, she inadvertently switched into his tatù and the force of it sent them both tumbling to the floor.

He gasped in surprise, then flipped them both over so he was lying on top of her, chuckling to himself as he smoothed back her hair. "No tatùs," he teased. "With Jennifer's, you could crush me in a second."

She giggled breathlessly as he began kissing her neck. "What?" she teased him back with a confidence she didn't know she possessed. "Afraid you wouldn't be up for the challenge?"

"Miss Kerrigan!" He pulled back for a second, flushed and grinning. "And here I thought you were a lady."

"I'm wearing a corset. It's easy to get confused."

They burst out laughing and pulled themselves together, kissing and laughing like no time at all had passed. It was sheer euphoria. Losing themselves in each other. Loving each other like there was nothing and no one in the world that could tear them apart.

Then all at once, they were up on the bed.

A shiver ran down Rae's spine as she tangled her fingers in Devon's hair. Was this really happening? How far were they going to go? Was she...was she ready for this?

It's a testament to how far gone they both were that neither of them heard someone walking up to the room. In fact, it wasn't until the door opened that either of them registered another person was there.

Both Rae and Devon shot away from each other at the speed of light, but Molly didn't need her tatù to see sparks. Her mouth fell open as the door swung shut behind her.

"Holy hot tarts!"

Chapter 3

It felt as if all the air had been sucked from the room. Rae's mouth opened and closed several times, like a fish gasping for oxygen, but no words came out. Devon stood as far away from her as he could, his back pressed against the wall. And from the look on his face, Rae was willing to bet he would have traded his fox tatù in a second if it meant he could become invisible.

"Molly," Rae finally started, "I can explain—"

Molly held one finger up, her eyes closed tight. "Don't!"

"If you'd just let me—"

"Nope!"

"But really," Devon said, trying his luck. "It isn't what it looks like—"

"Please." Molly finally cracked one eye open. "It's exactly what it looks like."

The three of them stood in silence for another minute. Devon staring at the ground, Molly staring at the ceiling, and Rae trying desperately to keep her slip from sliding down.

Finally, when it could go on no longer, Molly threw up her hands and broke the silence with an exasperated sigh. "Fish and chips."

Rae and Devon looked at her like she lost her mind.

"What?" Devon asked tentatively.

"If that's a new expletive you're trying out, I absolutely support you," Rae automatically volunteered.

Molly's eyes narrowed. "It's what we need. Food. A boost in blood sugar. Fuel for a second wind. A distraction from this...unbelievable secret you two have been hiding!" Her eyes fell on both of them critically, before resting on Rae. "And I need to have a talk with my best friend." She turned to Devon pointedly and cocked her head towards the hall. "*Alone.*"

"Got it." Devon started nodding so fast it looked like his head might detach as he backed away to the door. "Three fish and chips coming up. I'll bring them right back."

Still shaking her head, Molly made her way slowly to the bed, taking a seat with another ominous sigh.

Rae crossed the room slowly to join her, catching Devon's eye on the way out. *Don't you leave me with her*! she told him, using Molly's tatù.

Absentminded sparks shot from Molly's twitching hands.

Devon shrugged helplessly, but flashed her a grin and a mischievous wink as he vanished through the door. *She's your best friend*, he seemed to say. *Deal with it.*

The door clicked shut behind him and the two girls slowly faced one another, each one waiting for the other to speak. But just as Rae pulled in a deep breath to get started, Molly suddenly shrieked, "You and Devon!? You have got to be kidding me! This is...*so amazing*!"

Rae's mouth dropped open in shock. "That is...not what I was expecting you to say."

That was putting it mildly. Tatùs did not mix with other tatùs. It was absolutely forbidden and Molly had been indoctrinated in those rules just like the rest of them. Then again, if there was one thing Rae had learned about Molly, it was that she never ceased to surprise.

"*OW!*"

Rae flew off the bed with a giant shock and landed with a thud against the wall.

Case and point.

She got to her feet and rubbed a lump on the back of her head, thankful that Charles' tatù was already taking effect. "Yeah. That's more what I was expecting."

"How could you keep this from me?" Smoke was still swirling from Molly's fingers.

Rae stared at her friend before walking over to the dresser and pulling a shirt out to wear over her slipping slip. She kept a careful distance as she rejoined Molly on the bed. But just as she began to make her excuses, she forgot herself entirely and buried her face in her hands. She finally looked straight at her best friend. "It was *killing* me!" she wailed, rewarded by a startled look on Molly's face. "You have no idea how hard it was."

Molly's usual cheerful eyes flashed electricity. "I had no idea, because I'd never do that to you, Rae! I told you the first time I...you know...and you keep quiet as a church mouse!"

Rae's mind reeled back in shock as she realized where her friend was going. "Oh...oh no, no, no. No! We weren't going to... I mean, we weren't about to... I couldn't—"

"Spur of the moment thing, huh?" Molly nodded knowingly.

"No, it wasn't spur of the...well, I guess it was. But I wouldn't have actually gone through with it," Rae protested. "I'm not ready for that with anyone. I wouldn't have done *that*."

Inside, she wasn't so sure. Everything about being with Devon felt right. Natural. When they were together, it was somehow easy to forget the monumental difficulties of the last two years. With Devon, she didn't have to be Rae Kerrigan. She could just be Rae. The girl he met at Guilder. The one he said he'd fallen in love with.

The one he said he'd never stopped loving.

A tangled web of thoughts and emotions clouded her mind, crowding out all sense and reason. On this one thing, she was clear:

Devon loved her.

If nothing else ever happened, at least she had that.

She raised her eyes and stared across the bed to where her best friend waited impatiently for an explanation. Molly was right. It was time to come clean.

"I guess it started when I got to Guilder," she began quietly.

"No freaking way!" Molly interrupted loudly. "We were living together for Pete's sake! There is no way you kept that all from me! How could I have not seen it?"

Rae shook her head quickly. "No, we didn't get together right away, I mean...the connection was there from the start. I think Devon and I started falling in love all the way back in my first year at school."

"Love?" Molly raised her eyebrows so high they were in danger of disappearing into her hairline. "That's what we're talking about here? You two *love* each other?"

"I think so," Rae's voice came out almost a whisper. "He says he does, and I've never stopped loving him. It's just...complicated. Really complicated."

Molly snorted with laughter. "Yeah, I should say so! Not only is it completely illegal for two tatùs to date, but the both of you work for the Privy Council. It's not like it's going to be an easy secret to keep." Her face clouded momentarily. "Then again, you did keep it from me all these years..."

"Molly!" Rae's face crumpled in remorse. "You have to believe me—I wanted *nothing more* than to tell you. It was tearing me up inside, not having my best friend know. I just...I didn't know how you'd react." She hung her head. "You grew up in the world of tatùs, I didn't. These rules banning us have been pounded into your head since childhood—I just don't see it that way. Not to mention, I didn't want to risk you getting in trouble if Carter or anyone else were to find out."

Molly brought her hand up to her mouth, as if just realizing the gravity of their problem. "Oh...wow, that's right! How do you get away with it? I mean, with Carter's tatù and all? Can't he just touch your arm and know?"

Rae shook her head. "I've wondered that a lot. And to be honest, I'm still not entirely sure he doesn't. He's had plenty of opportunities when my guard has been down to probe hidden thoughts. And not just mine, but Devon's as well. I honestly couldn't tell you what he knows. Kraigan," she said, hating the name, "taught me one thing, he showed me how to block Carter's ability."

"Guess he isn't completely useless. Besides wanting you dead and all that." Molly got to her feet and started pacing, flicking her hand as if to push the thought if Kraigan away. "Rae, I don't know, this is just...just so unexpected. I mean, it's amazing, don't get me wrong. My best friend finally has a boyfriend! But...you and Devon? Most of the time I think you guys hate each other. You're always fuming or brooding or stomping off by yourselves." She suddenly shrugged. "Although, come to think of it, the two of you have always had a strange kind of connection. Like there was the world that all of us were living in, but then there was a different world as well—one with just the two of you."

Rae blinked in amazement at the unintentional profound nature of her statement. It was a perfect way to sum up her and Devon's relationship. It was a relationship of two worlds. One was blissful, free. Two people clearly meant for each other coming together in the most natural of ways. But the other world couldn't be more different. They lived under a microscope. Holding on to each other in the center of an ever-shrinking noose, just waiting for it to finally close in around them and end things once and for all. They didn't know who they could talk to, they didn't know who they could trust. In fact, in this other world—let's call it *reality*—Rae thought bitterly, she wasn't entirely sure she could even trust Devon.

"I don't know what to do," Rae said softly. "I know it's against the rules, but I can't help how I feel. The heart wants what it wants."

"Oh Rae..." Molly reached out her arms like she was going to hug her, but at the last second had a change of heart and smacked her in the shoulder.

"Okay Molls, you gotta pick an emotion here." Rae grimaced, rubbing her shoulder. "This whiplash is killing me."

"I just can't believe I didn't know!" Molly fumed. "I actually understand why you didn't tell me, but I don't know how I didn't pick up on it myself. I was *living* with you, and I had no idea."

Rea took a chance and flashed a mischievous smile. "Well, I am rather sneaky you know."

Molly laughed and threw a pillow her way. "Yes, Miss Kerrigan, you have completely outdone yourself. But enough is enough. You and Devon are together? Fine." Her eyes sparkled with scarcely contained merriment. "Now, you have to spill. Tell me everything!"

Over the last two years, there were dozens of times when Rae had imagined what it would be like to share her relationship with Molly. But not once, in all those imaginings, had she realized how much she actually *needed* to lean on her best friend.

She told her everything. Every detail, every question, every heartbreak. Every moonlit kiss and never-ending night when she had stared at her phone, waiting for him to text while he was undercover. How much it had hurt her to see him with another girl in their first year of school. How it had ripped at her heart to find him broken and bruised at the motel. How Devon's own father had specifically warned her to stay away.

By the time she had finished, even she had to admit they had a rather epic tale. But unfortunately, they could only live in one of the two worlds at once. Right now they were happy, blissful, in love. But it was only a matter of time before the other world, the real one, caught up with them. And Rae had absolutely no idea what either she or Devon would do when it did.

"Okay..." Molly said slowly, blinking as she absorbed an absurd amount of information in a short amount of time. To be honest, it was the longest Rae had ever heard her go without speaking while awake. "So that covers how you two got together, and then how he said it wouldn't work out, and you kind of fell apart. There's just one thing I don't understand."

Rae grabbed a hair band off her dresser and swept her remaining curls up into a ponytail. Devon must have been aiming for a fish and chips shop on the other side of London because she had been talking for nearly an hour and there was no sign of him.

"Just the one thing?" she asked teasingly. "That's a lot better than me, Molls. Shoot."

Molly crossed over to the dresser and tossed Rae a designer hoodie to zip over her t-shirt and bedraggled slip. Then she tossed her a pair of leggings. "I don't understand what happened tonight. You said you guys were broken up. But you sure didn't look very broken up to me when you were—"

"Okay, enough, I get the gist," Rae interrupted her.

Molly grinned and plopped back down on the bed. "So what happened? You two get carried away in the excitement of looking gorgeous tonight, or what?"

Rae sat down beside her and frowned thoughtfully as she considered. "I...I don't think so. It wasn't like tonight triggered something new, it's almost like...it pushed him over the edge? I think my being hurt might have unlocked something that was already there. Make sense?"

"Sure." Molly nodded seriously. "He thought he was going to lose you, so his true colors finally came out. Beating out the Privy Council, the world of tatùs, and even his own father." She flipped her hair casually. "It's actually not so uncommon. It happens in movies all the time."

Rae burst out laughing and pulled Molly into a tight hug. "I'm so glad I was finally able to tell you," she said sincerely between chuckles. "You're my best friend, Molls. You need to know."

Molly rolled her eyes. "You sure are the pot calling the kettle red!"

"Huh?" Rae shook her head, unsure of what Molly was saying.

"I would never have guessed goody-two-shoes you would fall for goody-two-shoes Devon."

"Ohhh..."

Molly, face completely serious, continued, "Leave it to you to fall in love with someone with a tatù, but at least you *finally* have someone you care about! I thought I was going to have to build you a sex-bot or something with MacGyver."

"What's a sex-bot?" Rae grimaced. "Gross!"

Just then, the door clicked and the two girls pulled away, still giggling, as Devon poked his head nervously into the room. "Knock, knock," he said tentatively, his eyes darting between the two of them. "Did I give you two enough time or am I going to get shocked when I come in here?"

Rae chuckled and rubbed the fading bump on her head. "You're safe. I took the shock that was meant for you about an hour ago."

Devon grinned. "Glad to hear it," he joked. Then he held up an oil-soaked paper bag. "I bought dinner. Hope you girls are hungry."

Molly hopped up from her seat on the bed and walked over to him. She eyed him up and down before snatching the bag away, planting her feet in front of him and standing eye to eye. Or—given their height different—eye to chin. "Devon Wardell, in the last two years, I've come to love you like a brother." She paused, editing. "I mean, a distant sort of brother with sometimes questionable fashion sense, but a brother nonetheless."

Devon tried to keep his face straight as he placed a warm hand on her shoulder. "Thanks Molls..."

"*That* being said." All at once Molly's face changed from angel to demon. "If you hurt my best friend, you're going to find out exactly what this tatù of mine can do." She wiggled her fingers ominously. "And I can assure you, it'll not be something you will easily forget. *If* you live."

"Understood." He tried to smile, but ended up taking a nervous step away. "Shall we eat in the kitchen?"

"Sounds great!" Just like that, Molly was all smiles again as she flounced off down the hall towards the dining room. "I'll grab utensils."

Devon watched her go with a baffled look in his eye before turning to Rae. "Does she always just..." He snapped his fingers. "Turn on a dime like that?"

Rae grinned and patted Devon's shoulder before heading down the hall. "Don't try to understand the complexities of the feminine mind," she advised. "It's beyond you mere mortals."

By the time the two of them got to the living room, the food was already plated and Molly had poured three glasses of orange juice. "Don't knock it," she warned as Devon eyed the juice skeptically, "you need your vitamins. They're good for the skin."

He muffled a snort of laughter and took a big swig as Rae sat down beside them. The food hit the spot. Salty and delicious. She hadn't even realized she was hungry, but before she knew it, she was kissing the last of the grease off her fingers and leaning back with a satisfied smile.

"Great call with the food," she thanked Molly.

Molly chomped down on a chip. "Someone has to keep track of these things. Do you realize that you two haven't eaten since breakfast? Rae—you're becoming nothing but cheekbones."

Rae laughed and slurped down the rest of her juice. It really had been a long day, and she was about to slip away and call it a night, when Molly suddenly leaned forward with a frown.

"So in all the excitement of catching you two *in the act*," she gave them both a devilish wink, "I totally forgot to ask. What on earth were you talking about with your mom?"

Upon hearing her question, Devon leaned forward as well and stared at Rae. He wanted the information too.

The sated fish and chips smile faded from Rae's face as she considered what to do. These days, it seemed impossible to know who to trust. Not only had she snuck off to Stoke on her own to find the key, she didn't know existed, but she had found out about the evidence locker from a member of the Xavier Knights—not exactly the easiest story to tell. At least Jennifer, her teacher, had kept the key a secret.

As she stared between both Molly and Devon's faces, she found herself reassured. They had both proven themselves, hadn't they? Time and time again. Who could she trust if not them?

She took a deep breath and spun her thumbs on the table in front of her. "I figured out the secret code and headed to Stoke. When I got to the Wade factory I found a key my mother had hidden in the old factory there. A key that Luke says matches an evidence box he found while going through my mom's file. Kraigan followed me, but I don't think he knew about the key. He didn't know my mom."

Molly frowned. "Wait—Luke? Why on earth would Luke know anything about it?"

Rae closed her eyes in a grimace. "Because he works for the Xavier Knights?"

"*What*?!"

"Keep going," Devon soothed Molly, urging Rae forward with his eyes.

"He's going to come here," Rae said. "He has the box, I have the key. And inside is the first ever concrete information I've been able to dig up on my mother. It could literally be the key to finding her."

Her two friends were silent for a moment, before Devon dropped his gaze. "And I stood in your way." He said it so softly he could have been speaking to himself.

Without thinking, Rea reached out and squeezed his hand. "You didn't know."

"Wait a minute," Molly said loudly, oblivious to their exchange, "could this evidence box have anything to do with that note and the code we found? Was that the secret code?" She slammed her hand on the table in triumph. "I knew it went to a lock box!"

"Hold up," Devon leaned forward again, "what note? What code?"

Molly shushed him excitedly. "If you intentionally remove yourself from Rae's life for any amount of time, you're going to miss big things. Enormous things always happen when she's around. She found a hidden note from her mom, it had a secret code. And I'm a master spy. Keep up."

Rae shook her head and grinned. "The note led me to the factory, but it burned up in the fire before I could decipher any more of it. All I know, is that it led me to the key." All at once, she struck her forehead as she remembered. "The key...it's back in my room at Guilder." *Great thinking Rae, you'd go to meet Luke and get the box, and then what? Smuggle it back to school?*

"So what's the plan?" Molly asked, grabbing the plates and stuffing them into the dishwasher.

"I guess I hadn't thought that far ahead." Rae's brows pressed together. "I just found out there was a box when Luke called me, and with the soon-to-be princess getting attacked and everything...I forgot the key isn't here."

"But the box is." Devon looked at her with sudden determination.

"And it's not even midnight," Molly took over, "and Guilder is only an hour's drive away."

"It's more than an hour," Rae said.

"Not if Devon's driving." Molly nodded her head in his direction.

Rae stared back and forth between her two friends, not understanding their abrupt shift in dynamic. Molly's eyes shone as she rocked back and forth on the edge of her seat. Even Devon had set his jaw in that way he did when he made up his mind to do something.

"Whoa, what are you guys thinking?" Rae tried to temper them. "Carter told me point blank I couldn't go. I can't risk you guys getting in trouble by breaking rules."

"I'm not suggesting we break any rules," Molly said innocently. "You two are the rule-breakers here, not me. I'm only repeating what you already told him."

Rae grinned as a warm hum began coursing through her veins. "Yeah? And what's that?"

"You said you'd be back by breakfast..."

Chapter 4

"You have got to be kidding me."

Molly, Devon, and Rae crouched in the bushes across the sweeping lawns of Guilder. The moon hung high above them, bathing the ground in silvers and violets, and all around them, the sounds of night snapped and fluttered in the breeze. After the clamor of London and the attack at the ball, it was refreshingly peaceful. The kind of night Rae had learned to treasure at her school.

Except that tonight...she and her friends had other plans.

Rae stared up at the high, stone walls, above which her little window sat darkened against the sky. What had once seemed like a majestic, almost castle-like tower, now looked insurmountable.

"Why can't I just go in through the door again?"

Molly fidgeted excitedly in the tall grass and stuffed more of her vibrant hair up into her beanie. "Because it's locked and it's not like Devon could just go and ask Carter for the key. Plus, if you broke in, everyone would hear."

"Maybe not," Rae said hopefully, eyeing the three story drop. "Maybe I could do it really, really quietly..."

Molly raised her eyebrows doubtfully. "Quiet enough not to wake Madame Elpis? I don't think so. Now go, you big baby, it's not that far."

"Not that far?" Rae hissed under her breath. "If I fall it's going to take more than Charles' healing tatù to save me."

"Well, short of you just popping into a bird and flying on up there, it's the only way. Hang on," Molly's eyes grew suddenly wide, "you can't do that, can you?!"

"No." Rae bristled defensively. "Not anymore," she added under her breath.

"Well, I don't see why I can't go," Devon countered through his teeth. "There's no reason why Rae has to be the one to take the risk."

Molly shook her head. "Devon, it's adorable you feel so protective, but I hate to say it—and this is in no way an attack on your manliness—but with Jennifer's tatù, Rae's stronger than you. You might be able to cross the lawn in a blur, but when it comes to climbing, Rae's our best bet."

"I'm sure I'd be fine," he muttered. "Increased agility and all."

Molly rolled her eyes and nudged Rae. "Come on girlie, you're up."

Rae took a deep breath and got to her feet, brushing leaves and grass from her pants as she eyed the distance between where they were hiding and the Aumbry House wall. "Okay," she breathed to herself, "you can do this." She was about to take off when Molly suddenly grabbed her arm.

"Wait! Remember your spy gear!"

Rae threw up her hands as Devon rolled his eyes in the background. "Molly, I know that you're new to the Privy Council and everything, but it's not really about the—"

"How would you know?" Molly asked importantly. "Are you the PC's official stylist?" She stared her friends down with a smug smile. "Yep—that's what I thought. Now," she snapped her fingers and gestured for Rae to take the black beanie she was offering, "spy gear."

Deciding it was easier not to fight her, Rae snatched the hat out of her hand and clamped it down over her head. Upon Molly's extreme insistence, the three of them were already decked out head to toe in black. The same sort of fitted jumpsuits she had worn with Julian when breaking into the museum. And while they might look right at home in some black ops espionage film, Rae could not have felt more ridiculous wearing it to break into her own dorm room.

"Fine," she caved, pulling out her long dark ponytail and letting it spill down her back. "But if this thing catches on a rock or something, it's on your head, stylist. Not mine."

"Technically, it would be on the rock." Molly pushed her forward. "Now go!"

Without pausing to think about the ramifications of what she was doing, Rae took off into the dark night. The wide, sweeping lawns she'd walked a million times were suddenly a ticking time bomb. Sure it was dark, and she was fast as the wind and—yes Molly—wearing black, but none of the people at Guilder were to be underestimated. There were people who could hear things from miles away, spot things at ten thousand yards, even some who could camouflage into the trees.

She cast a suspicious look at an elm as she flew by, finally reaching the base of the wall beneath her window. Even from this distance, she could clearly see the trees where her two friends were hiding with the help of her tatù. Molly was speed-talking a mile a minute, but Devon was staring straight back at her, seeing her as clearly as she could see him. She flashed him a quick smile and a thumbs up before turning back to the wall.

Now for the tricky part. She squinted up into the night sky. The climb.

Switching back into Jennifer's tatù for strength, she searched around until she found a good grip for both her hands. Then she started, ever-so-slowly, working her way up the wall.

It didn't take long for her to realize she was in trouble.

While she had no problem lifting up her body, the stones of Guilder had worn smooth over the decades of rain, wind, and snow. The higher she climbed, the harder it was to find a workable grip, and once or twice, she had to pull herself up using just her fingers. *Devon was right. I should have let him do this. He's probably done it a million times.*

And so it continued. One foot after another. One trembling hand above the one before. But despite the difficulty of the climb, it seemed like luck was on her side. The moon had thankfully slipped behind some clouds, shrouding her in darkness, and she had yet to hear a single thing besides shallow, sleeping breathing from inside. After what felt like an eternity, she was within sight of the window.

That was where her luck ran out.

There were no cracks in the stone. No little grooves to put her hands. *Nothing.*

Panicked, she glanced above her and tried to get her bearings. She was in a straight line below her window; she could almost see the cracking paint on the ledge. However, the stone between them wasn't cobbled like the rest. It was a sheer slab of gray granite. Completely smoothed over without a single imperfection for her to use to get up.

Okay Rae, just think.

She breathed in through her nose and out through her mouth, trying to calm herself down. There had to be something she could do. Some useful tatù she could use. She browsed quickly through her roster but came up flat. Damn Kraigan! If he hadn't drained her of some of her favorite abilities, she could have just turned into an eagle and flown in through the open glass. In and out in five minutes. Plus, she wouldn't have had to put up with Molly's silly spy gear.

She made a mental note to gather more tatùs as quickly as possible and focused once more on the ledge. What could she use...? Ice? Wind? Maybe if she made a big enough gust, she could literally blow herself inside. Granted, she had never used the power in such a directed way and was pretty sure it didn't work like that.

Think Rae, think!

But inside, she knew the truth. These days her body picked the tatù before she did, selecting whatever would be most helpful in her current situation. It was staying with Jennifer's—relying on its strength to make sure she didn't fall.

Jennifer's it would have to be then.

Using every ounce of determination she had, she tried a tentative jump for the window. Big mistake! She only leapt up about a foot or two, before she fell back down the wall, hands flailing frantically for a hold. She caught herself with one hand and quickly made up the distance she had lost, but her original problem remained. There was simply no way to make it to the ledge.

"Whatchya doing?"

Rae almost slipped off the wall, stifling a shriek in her arm before staring up into the darkness. Julian was leaning out of her window frame, casually munching on a bag of crisps. She had never been so happy to see him. Or so ready to kill him.

"You having fun? Sightseeing?" he asked in the same teasing manner. "It's a long way down, be a shame if you fell..."

A wide grin spread over Rae's face even as she tried to make it look serious. "Could you stop messing around and pull me in? And wipe your hands off," she commanded, eyeing the crisps. "I don't want to fall to my death because you had greasy fingers."

Julian grinned and wiped his hands on his pants before leaning as far out of the window as he could and reaching for her hand. She stretched up into the night and grasped onto his fingers, hoisting herself even higher to get a good grip.

Julian didn't have a strength tatù like she did, but he was naturally fit and strong. With what seemed like very little effort, he pulled her in through the open window and set her down gently on the floor. The second she was grounded, she leapt upon him in a huge hug.

"Okay," he laughed, "it's good to see you too Rae." She held on tight and felt a tremor run through his body. *"Okay,"* he sounded slightly strained, "too hard—a little too hard."

She pulled away, still smiling. "You saw me?"

He brushed his long hair out of his face and sat down on her bed. "I was walking back to my room after some late night training, when this image flashed through my head." He gave her a once over and smirked. "Covert Barbie hanging from the third story wall."

Rae snorted sarcastically. "So you came running to my rescue?"

"No," he picked up the crisps, "I saw I had a little time, so I grabbed a snack."

She laughed and shook her head. "Very pragmatic."

Same old Julian. Always there when you needed him, but with a twist.

"So what's up, Rae?" He watched, his head slightly tilted to the side. "I also saw Devon and Molly hiding out in the bushes, but I decided to come here first." His eyes lit up with their familiar sparkle as he crumpled the bag and threw it into her trash. "What's the mission?"

If it were anyone else asking, Rae would have made up an instant excuse. But in many ways, Julian was the person she trusted most in the world. He had never lied to her or blabbed a secret without thinking. He was open and honest. A true friend. She would be as well.

"I found a key at that factory in Stoke," she said softly. "Turns out it goes to a lock box with some clues about whatever it was that happened to my mom. The box is in London, but I forgot the key back here." She stared hesitantly up at his face. "It's not exactly a sanctioned mission."

He nodded once and smiled. "Understood. So where is it?"

Rae shook her head, baffled by the inherent goodness of Julian. Without saying a word, she cocked her head towards a case of porcelain figurines. He followed her gaze and strode across the room to open it, pausing as he glanced over the miniature army of animals.

"It's not the schnauzer, is it?"

Rae giggled. "It's a key. It's there on the side."

"Got it." He took it carefully in his long fingers and dropped it in her hand. "This is so cool, Rae," he said with sincere excitement. "You can finally get some answers about your mom."

Rae's eyes teared automatically and she grabbed him for another quick hug before slipping the key into her pocket. "Thank you," she said softly.

He chuckled and glanced out the window. "I like making Devon sweat by thinking I've got the hots for you. Plus, I couldn't just let you fall."

She shook her head. "No," she traced the outline of the key in her jeans, "for understanding. For being you."

A soft smile lit his face and he gave her a wink. "Don't mention it. Now go get 'em champ. I'll hold down the fort."

She grinned and clapped him on the shoulder, before they both returned to the window ledge and gazed down. It was hard enough getting up. How on earth was Julian supposed to lower her back down so that she could find a grip? Dangle her by her shoes?

She needn't have worried. The second they leaned their heads over the frame, they saw Devon hanging there in the dark.

"Told you I'd come in handy."

Rae could see his dimple even from where she stood. She grinned.

"What did he say?" Julian asked, squinting down towards the grass.

Rae rolled her eyes. "He's boasting about being useful."

Julian laughed softly. "Sounds like Devon. Also sounds like...you two might be on again?"

She smacked his shoulder. "What? Did you draw that too?"

"Nope." He tapped his head. "Just my God-given intuition. It must have been some ball."

Rae rolled her eyes and jumped up into his arms. "You have no idea. I'll have to tell you all about it when we get back."

"Can't wait." He held her out the open window. "And before you say anything—I already know. *You were never here*." He gave her a wink and then dropped her in mid-air.

She resisted the urge to scream as she fell silent as a stone through the night, landing a second later in Devon's warm arms.

"Geez," she whispered, pressing her face into his neck, "next time, how about we make Molly climb?"

Devon grinned. "Sounds like a plan."

She shifted to hop down, but before she could, he took off sprinting into the night, holding her against his chest like a teddy bear. She could feel his heart pounding through his shirt and smiled to herself as she nestled in, enjoying the brief seconds it took him to return to the woods. After going without it for however long, it was something she would never take for granted again. The beautiful sound of Devon's rhythmic heart.

Before she'd nearly had her fill, she was back on solid ground.

"So did you find it?" Molly asked the second Rae's shoes touched dirt.

"Sure did." Rae rummaged in her pocket and pulled out the key. "Next stop, London."

Even though they were only about an hour from the pub, both Rae and Molly took the time in the taxi to get a little sleep. They had purposely left Devon's car at Heath Hall, hoping that if anyone came by to check on them, it would look like they'd stayed in for the night. Rae had texted Luke before they'd gone, apologizing for the late hour, but asking that he meet her anyway and bring the box. He had eagerly complied—too eagerly for Rae's taste and she felt guilty. Just a few hours ago he'd risked his whole job just to help her, and then she went and kissed Devon. Not only that, but now she was bringing Devon along with her to the meeting, a fact she'd conveniently left out when making plans with Luke. She wasn't sure how either boy would react to the other, but it was a thought she'd put off as long as possible.

When the taxi pulled up at the curb, Devon shook her and Molly awake. "We're here," he said, pulling out a stack of bills and handing them to the driver.

"Already?" Molly stretched noisily and looked around. "Geez, it's really dead out here."

"It's two in the morning," Devon reminded her as she crawled outside, followed closely by a yawning Rae.

The brisk night air bit at their faces and Rae pulled her dark jacket tighter around her, secretly glad Molly had insisted on it. A neon light flashed intermittently above their heads, occasionally zapping a fly or mosquito who got too close. *Charming*, Rae thought. The pub was called Second Sister, a name which she silently pondered as they walked inside.

They were greeted immediately with a strong whiff of stale beer and peanuts. There were only a few patrons and a single bartender. Perfect for the kind of discreet meeting Rae had in mind.

She spotted Luke immediately, playing with an empty beer pint as he waited patiently at the bar. As if by chance, he glanced over his shoulder and spotted her at the same time. He jumped off the stool and moved towards her, a bright smile lighting his face. Before she could stop him, he scooped her up in a tight hug, holding on a second longer than was necessary, his hands lingering on her back. She gasped a little with the strength of it as he set her lightly down on her feet.

"Luke, it's so good to see you." She tried to smile as brightly as him, but an ominous sort of guilt had started tugging away at her stomach.

"It's great seeing you too!" He beamed then took a small step back and gave them all a once-over. "I'm sorry, was I supposed to dress like Jason Bourne too?"

Molly turned to Rae and whispered excitedly. "See! I told you we looked like Bourne!"

Rae shushed her and turned back to Luke. "You're fine. Thanks again for meeting me so late. I really appreciate it."

Luke flashed her a warm smile, his blond hair catching the dim light. "It's no problem." His eyes wandered over her and Molly and then seemed to register Devon's presence for the first time. His smile faded slightly. "Who's this?"

Devon's face was hard, but he extended a polite hand. "Devon Wardell. Privy Council."

Luke glanced at the hand but folded his arms across his chest. "Sorry if I don't shake. Never know what tatù a person is carrying, you know?"

Rae blanched, her mind flashing back to the bear hug he'd just given her. He sure didn't seem to have a problem with tatùs then...or touching.

"Wardell?" Luke repeated, looking Devon up and down. "I know all about you." His lips thinned into a flat smile. "The Xavier Knights keep files on everybody."

Devon smiled back, but a muscle twitched at his jaw. "That's right, you're their file-boy."

Luke's eyes flashed. "What's that supposed to mean?"

"Just that it seems really...convenient. How you came into Rae's life the moment she joined up with the PCs."

"Certainly." Luke fought to keep his composure. "I always thought it had to be really nice for her. Spending time with someone without worrying about breaking the rules. I know how you tatùs aren't supposed to mix, and how you are so gung-ho about following the rules."

Devon took a sudden step forward. "I don't know exactly what you're insinuating, but—"

"*And*...that's enough." Molly popped up in between them, pushing them apart with crackling, electric hands. "Why don't we all just calm down before someone accidently gets electrocuted?" She tossed her hair over her shoulders and flashed a lethal, but charming smile. "I believe we all came here for a specific reason. Why don't we get a booth?"

"No need." Luke gritted his teeth. "Sorry Rae, but I'm not giving you the box with Wardell here."

Rae's mouth fell open. She couldn't believe he was being so openly hostile. They weren't dating. They hadn't even kissed! And this was much, much bigger than any sort of testosterone fueled rivalry. This was about finding her freaking mom! "*What*?" The word hissed out with more venom than she had intended. "Luke, we're talking about my *mother*. It has nothing to do with Devon. Give me the damn box!"

Luke pretended to scoff. "It's nothing personal, I just don't feel comfortable revealing Xavier Knight information with a member of the Privy Council around."

There was a beat of silence before Rae actually stamped her foot in frustration. "*I'm* a member of the Privy Council."

Luke nodded calmly. "But I trust you."

"And I trust Devon. And Molly."

For a minute the four of them stood there at an impasse—the girls frowning in confusion as the boys stared each other down. Rae honestly didn't know what to do. She hadn't expected the boys to like each other, but she certainly hadn't expected anything like this. There was not an inch of compromise on either of their faces. And the three of them had to be back by morning. They were running out of time.

"Look, this is getting us nowhere," Molly finally said. "Why don't Devon and I wait in that booth in the corner, and you can give Rae the box?"

Devon rolled his eyes in disgust, but Rae looked at Luke eagerly—hoping he would find the terms acceptable. What she saw wasn't encouraging.

"That's...not quite going to work." Luke shifted his weight uncomfortably and Rae actually threw up her hands in exasperation.

"*Why*? Look, you said you trusted me, right? Well, you're just going to have to trust me now."

"No, I know, it's just not that simple. You see, it's not exactly here...with me."

Rae put her hands on her hips impatiently. "Well where the hell is it?"

Luke glanced at her apologetically before he turned to Devon with a bright, almost triumphant grin. "It's at my apartment."

Chapter 5

"Abso-freaking-not!"

Rae pawed the ground nervously with her shoe. "Devon—"

"There's no way in hell you're going to that guy's apartment with him." He turned his raging eyes away from her and fixed them on Luke. "Slick move, considering you thought she'd be alone."

"Just hold up guys." Molly tried to calm everyone. "I'm sure there's a reasonable explana—"

"Hey man, I would never do anything to hurt Rae." A flaming crimson flushed Luke's cheeks. "I didn't bring the box here because it contains proprietary Xavier Knights information. Aside from the fact that I didn't want my boss to find out and lose my job," he stared down Devon with just as much accusatory venom, "I was worried about it falling into the wrong hands."

"Whose?" Devon growled "Those hands would be mine?"

Tiny blue flames shot from Rae's fingers and the three of them fell suddenly quiet. Devon glared at Luke, Luke glared at Devon, and Molly stared back at Rae with wide, supportive eyes.

"This is not about what either of you think." Rae's voice had never been so deadly. "It's not about how you feel. It's not about who you woke up this morning and decided to trust." She crossed her arms over her chest and stared both boys square in the eyes as little warning trails of smoke spiraled from her palms. "This is about me and my mother. That's all there is to it."

A crumpled man who had to have been a least two hundred years old stared in drunken amazement at her hands and she quickly stuffed them into her pockets. There was no time left to waste here. They only had a few hours before they were supposed to be back at Heath Hall.

"Devon, you and Molly are going to wait here while Luke and I go to his apartment to get the box." She held up a hand to stop his automatic protest. "If I'm not back in exactly one hour, you can call out the cavalry. Luke'll give you his address before we go."

"Rae," Devon's voice was pleading, "I don't think this is the best—"

"If you don't think I can hold my own against one guy." She glanced at Luke in irritation about his sudden bias towards her world. "Especially a guy who doesn't even have a tatù, then you clearly don't know me very well."

Devon nodded shortly, finally appeased, while Luke's cheeks flushed a deeper embarrassed red.

"Molly," Rae continued, "keep your phone on and don't fall asleep. If there's any trouble or anything out of the ordinary, I'll give you a shout."

She nodded very seriously then grabbed Devon's arm and pulled him towards a booth in the corner. "Come on, you jealous dork. You're buying me about a million coffees so I can stay awake."

Once the two of them were alone, Rae turned to Luke and eyed him warily. "I better not be making a big mistake here," she warned. "I thought you were going to come with the box."

Luke nodded apologetically and held open the door as they made their way out into the night. "That was the original plan. But after I got your texts, I got an automated email from the company server saying that because of the specific nature of my search, an inquiry was being sent to corporate headquarters."

Rae raised her eyebrows. It made the Xavier Knights sound like a Fortune 500. "Let me guess, voice identification and retinal scans?" Luke shot her a strange look and she dropped her eyes to the cement. She must be spending too much time with Molly.

"I imagine it's something like what you're used to with the PC."

Rae stuffed her hands into her pockets and sighed, well aware of the hot-tempered mess she was leaving behind her in the bar. "Maybe it's best if we just avoid that whole subject right now."

Luke moved like he was going to put his hand on her shoulder but thought better of it. "I'm sorry." He sounded sincere. "You know I couldn't care less whether someone has a tatù or not, I was just frustrated. I didn't meant to cause trouble for you...and your boyfriend, if that's what he is now. I just can't bring myself to trust anyone that associates with the PCs." He nudged her playfully. "You're my one exception. Well," he snorted, "you and Molly. I couldn't imagine her staying quiet long enough to keep many secrets."

"You'd be surprised," Rae admitted. "I think she's better at this covert spy stuff than anyone gives her credit for." They walked in silence for another moment before she added, "And he's not my boyfriend. I mean, not really. It's..." She sighed. "It's complicated."

Luke nodded to himself, shooting her a sideways grin. "Caught that, did you?"

She couldn't help but grin. "Yeah, turns out subtlety isn't one of your strong suits."

"I'll have to work on it." They came to a crossroads and Luke pointed up the street to a row of nice-looking apartments just around the bend. "Right up there. Close enough to run back to the bar if I do anything *untoward*. It's a Xavier Knight's apartment but nobody knows I'm there. I promise. I'm risking everything to bring this to you."

Rae shook her head and chuckled. "Don't knock how protective Devon and Molly are. You would be too if you were in their shoes. I've had some pretty close calls in the last two years with people I've grown to trust. People that ended up betraying me."

"I *am* protective." Luke brought her to a sudden stop and stared down at her in the bright moonlight. "And I'm seriously worried Devon's one of those people you'll come to regret."

Rae's eyes flashed. "You don't even know him. You don't know a thing about him."

"I know that he's one of the fastest rising agents the PC has ever seen," Luke replied. "I know that his father's the headmaster at your school. I know that he was assigned to be your mentor your first year in. For the last two years, he's been perfectly positioned to gain your trust."

Rae's breath billowed out in a nervous cloud in front of her. How could he possibly know all that information from a Xavier Knight file? Where were they getting all this information? That Devon was her mentor her first year at Guilder—how many people could have even known that? It was a pretty limited pool. And for the Knights to have the information, it had to mean...

"You've got a rogue agent," Luke finished her dark thought.

Panicked, but well aware of their time constraints, Rae took Luke's arm and forced them to keep moving. If there really was a mole in the PC, it could have been either Lanford or Kraigan. There was no reason to think that someone was currently acting against them.

"Let me ask you something," she said as they walked up a cobblestone path to the front door, "this file you read on Devon...when was it created?"

Luke gave her a serious look as though he knew what she was thinking. "That's the thing, Rae. They're being constantly updated as new information comes in. It's not just speculation based on the past—someone is actively adding to them."

"But not Devon." The words were out of her mouth before she could stop them. "He would just never do that. There's no way. I've never met anyone more loyal to the Privy Council." *Trust me. It's becoming a huge problem.*

Luke looked like he wanted to say something else, but instead he just pulled out his keys and shrugged. "If you say so." He sounded skeptical. "It's your life. I trust you to know who to have confidence in."

Although she was touched by the vote of assurance, Rae shook her head wearily. "That's like the question of the year, isn't it? Who to trust? I feel like I'm constantly asking that question. Treating my friends like suspects." She glanced up at him. "Building up walls against new people."

"Hey," he knelt down suddenly and took both her hands, "if there's someone who deserves to be a little defensive, it's you. Think about what you've been through in the last few years." He straightened up and shook his head in amazement. "Remember, I've read your file too."

He pushed the door open and Rae was hit in the face with the overwhelming smell of household cleaners. "Whoa," she took a step back, bringing her hand up over her mouth, "did you bring Windex here to die?"

He laughed in a rush of nervous energy. "Sorry. When I knew you'd be coming here tonight, I didn't want any clues of anyone or anything to catch me, or you. I'm afraid I might have gone a little overboard rushing to get things hospitable."

Rae giggled as she stepped inside. "Well, it's very...clean." Actually, when she looked around, it was a pretty awesome apartment.

The first thing she noticed were the floor to ceiling bookshelves—something she'd seen once in a magazine and always wanted in her own house. They were stacked high with everything from classic poetry to sci-fi adventures. She trailed her fingers across their stiff spines as her eyes wandered around the room. It was a man's house, there was no denying it. The colors and furniture were classic male. But there was a welcoming air to it as well. A softness that left room for further interpretation. In short, it was a great apartment just waiting for a female touch.

Luke shuffled his feet nervously in the corner, waiting for her verdict. "Well?" he finally asked, watching as she examined an unused blender.

"It's great," she said brightly, looking up with a grin. "Actually, it's exactly the kind of place Molly and I are hoping to get in a few months."

"Really? I decorated this one!"

Rae couldn't tell if he was excited that she approved, or excited that the person she was moving in with was Molly and not Devon.

"So that's going to be after your graduation?" he asked, leading her to the kitchen and turning on an antique coffee maker. Rae glanced around the cupboards and pulled out two mugs, setting them down beside him.

"Yep. We want to be somewhere close enough to get to work, but still within the city limits. It's such a new idea, I actually haven't really gotten a chance to think it through." She closed her eyes in a sudden grimace. "Like what a little tyrant Molly is going to be about decorating."

Luke chuckled and began pouring their drinks. "It can't be that bad..."

Rae shook her head. "You have no idea. You should have seen when she joined up with the Privy Council and became a *spy*. Her whole vocabulary and wardrobe shifted accordingly. I can only imagine what her inner decorator will look like."

She mentally braced herself for marathons of extreme home makeover as she took a scalding gulp of coffee. The caffeine instantly revived her, making it feel a bit like she'd switched to Riley's cheetah tatù. Luke clinked his mug against hers and downed half of it in one gulp.

This was nice, she couldn't help but think. Coffee in the kitchen. Casual conversation about normal topics. Not running around the countryside dodging psychopaths and burning things down.

But that wasn't why she was here.

With a brisk smile, she set the mug on the counter. "Enough about my impending tutorial on Feng shui. Can I see the box?"

Luke's smile faltered for a second before he set down his mug as well. "Sure. It's in here."

He led her back to the living room and she took a seat as he rummaged through his bag. A second later, he pulled out a small brass case, about the size of a shoe box. Rae's heart leapt as he set it down on the coffee table in front of her. It was the same kind of dulled brass as the key.

"Would you...?" Rae looked up in surprise to see Luke hovering near the door. "Would you like me to step out for a minute so you can go through it by yourself?"

"Oh..." Rae paused, she hadn't considered that possibility. Her mind raced with a dozen pros or cons, but she silenced them all and looked up in Luke's face with a calm smile. "No, please stay." Their eyes met. "I trust you."

His whole face seemed to shine as he returned the smile and took a seat beside her. "I'm glad to hear it," he said softly. Then a little louder, "You ready to do this?"

Rae took a deep breath. "Only one way to find out."

She turned the key in the lock and opened the lid with gentle fingers, careful not to disturb the contents of the box. Then both she and Luke held their breath and slowly leaned forward as they peered inside. If Rae was hoping for a family heirloom, five secret passports, or a stack of baby photos, she was sadly mistaken. All there was inside was a thin stack of papers and an old VCR camcorder. She leaned back against the cushion, feeling almost let down.

Her mother's entire legacy fit in a shoe box.

Then she set her jaw in determination and lifted out the papers. It was one shoe box more than she'd had yesterday. She'd take it.

"What are the papers?" Luke asked curiously, leaning back to give her a little space.

Rae flipped through them with a concentrated frown. "They look like files of some kind...all with her picture posted on top..." Her fingers traced the photo as she scanned down to read the rest. "Wait a minute—these are missions! A record of all of the missions she went on for the PC!"

Luke peeked over her shoulder and made a low whistle. "Your mom broke in to the Empire State Building? I'm seriously impressed."

Rae's face glowed as she soaked in all the precious details. "Yeah, well it sounds like she was seriously impressive."

"Like her daughter." Luke gave her a soft nudge.

Rae blushed but kept reading. "There's something else here too—a marriage certificate." Her face paled as she looked at her father's handwriting. "It said the ceremony was carried out by Father Amos at St. Stephen's Church, right here in London." She looked at Luke eagerly. "I wonder if he's still there."

"Maybe." Luke pulled out the camcorder with a frown. "Geez, I haven't seen one of these things in ages." He pushed eject and a cassette popped out into his hand.

Rae sucked in a deep breath, almost afraid to hope. "You don't happen to have a VCR, do you?"

"My dear, you underestimate me." He got to his feet and pulled back the sliding door on his entertainment stand. "I always keep one for times such as these."

He slid in the tape and rejoined her on the couch, giving her shoulder a comforting squeeze as he settled in beside her. She scooted to the edge of the cushion and kept her eyes fixed on the screen. She couldn't believe it. Any second now, there was a chance she was going to see...

Mom.

The static cleared onto a beautiful face—a face Rae had seen pieces of while looking in the mirror for as long as she could remember. She felt like if she closed her eyes, she could already draw it from memory, but she didn't dare look away. If she looked away, her mother might not be there smiling at her when she looked back.

"Hello my darling."

Two silent tears slipped down Rae's cheeks. She knew that voice. She could swear she felt the tatù on her lower back warming in reply.

"My sweet, sweet Rae. If you're watching this, it means I'm not there to tell you these things in person. And for that, I am truly sorry. This world is not a safe place, I'm afraid you'll grow to learn that lesson better than anyone. All I can do now is equip you the best I can. And so, my dear daughter, there are some things you need to know."

The video had been recorded in the kitchen of their old house. Rae recognized the curtains blowing in through the sunny window. The first blossoms of spring could just barely be seen popping up outside. This had to have been made just a few months before the fire.

"Things are happening, Rae. Both inside the Privy Council and out. It's getting harder and harder to know who to trust. Too many locked doors and hushed meetings. I feel like something big is about to happen, I just don't know what."

She tucked a stray lock of hair behind her ear and Rae silently mimicked the same gesture. *So that's where that came from...*

"I've been gathering files. Not just my mission reports, look deeper Rae. I know you know how."

Rae's breath caught in her chest as she remembered the code and the secret language. She did know how. She just had to remember. There must be more to those files than met the eye.

A distinct sound of gravel on tires in the video made Beth jump around with a start. When she turned back, her eyes were panicked and she spoke faster than before.

"Rae listen to me, I don't have a lot of time. There's something else. Some big project your father is working on. I keep hearing him say something about the *device*. But what's more is that I don't think I'm the only person undercover here. There have been too many slip ups. Too many leaks that no one can explain. I think someone else close to us is leaking information. I think there's a mole in the Privy Council."

Rae felt like she was watching the video through a tunnel—trying desperately to keep focused on what her mother was saying, when in reality, she just wanted to freeze the image and stare at her face. An intermittent creaking sound kept interrupting the feed—something Rae felt like she should know but couldn't quite place.

"This is unbelievable," she whispered suddenly, covering her face in her hands.

"What is it?" Luke asked anxiously, rubbing her back in concern.

"That sound in the background is the swing set. I'm playing outside."

He opened his mouth in silent horror and they both turned back to the tape. Her mother was half on her feet now, leaning in to the camera as quick footsteps walked in from outside.

"Rae the thing is, I don't think the mole is working for the Xavier Knights or anybody else that's on our radar," Beth whispered frantically, glancing over her shoulder. "Honey, you're not going to believe this, no one is, but I think I know the person behind all of this. By now, chances are, you've probably heard of them too. It's—"

There was a grating screech in the VCR followed by a sharp acidic smell.

And just like that...the tape was gone.

Chapter 6

For a minute, it seemed everything froze.

The room went instant quiet. Enough that you could hear the second hand of Luke's watch slowly ticking away as smoke spiraled up from the VCR.

Then everything inside Rae exploded.

"What the hell happened?!" Her shrill screech echoed in the tiny room. "Get it back!"

Luke got to his feet and ran to the VCR in a flash. When he pushed up the flap to retrieve the tape, the burning smell of molten plastic hit their nostrils. He yelped and pulled back his hand, waving it through the air to cool the burn.

"I have no idea why it did that," he said in astonishment. "This machine's old, but it's brand new."

"It just ate my tape! The only video I have of my mom!" Tears spilled down Rae's cheeks as she sunk to her knees in front of the broken machine. "Can you fix it? Please, *please* fix it, Luke! I need to get it back." Her fingers reached up towards the screen. "I need to see her again! I can't—"

"Hey." Soft hands caught her and drew her into a gentle embrace. She didn't know how long she sat there, sobbing wildly into his chest as the image of her mother slowly faded into black.

She had been there. *Right* there. And now, Rae didn't know if she would ever see her again. She should have used her bloody phone and videoed it at the same time. Why hadn't she thought of that? It probably had some inside mechanism to self-destruct.

When she finally pulled herself together and caught her breath, she looked up to see Luke staring down at her with tender concern. She hastily wiped the tears from her face, and couldn't resist the nagging guilty feeling when he stroked the back of her hair. She pulled away quickly. "Thanks," she muttered, straightening herself up, "sorry about that."

"You don't have to apologize," Luke exclaimed. He hadn't moved from his position on the floor, silently allowing her to come back if she wished. "You just saw your freakin' *mother*. I understand the tears."

"It's not just that." Rae acknowledged the real source of her pain as she put it to words. "She didn't say anything about—" Her voice cracked and she took another second to calm herself down. "She didn't give any indication she might be in hiding. What if she's not alive? This could all be just me desperately hoping. I mean, if she really was, wouldn't she have come back to get me? She loved me. She wouldn't have left me."

The truth settled around her like a dense fog.

She sighed. "I thought I'd open the box and find out that she was out there somewhere, waiting for me." She laughed derisively at her hopes. "I half expected an address, for Pete's sake." More tears fell down her face, but she ignored them as she stared grimly out the window. "I'm an idiot."

"Rae," Luke took her hands again, "you're *not*. For the last few years, your world has been turning on a dime almost daily. First, you find out that you belong to this secret world of people with supernatural abilities. Then, you find out that your parents did too. Then, you find out that your dad was a madman and you have a half-brother who wants to kill you."

Rae shook her head at the surreal absurdity of what he was saying.

He squeezed her wrist. "All I'm saying is you're entitled to a healthy bit of doubt. You're well within your right to refuse to take things at face value." He pulled back and looked at her squarely. "Why did you think your mom might still be alive? You have to have a good reason."

"In truth?" Rae sighed and opened up her palm. "Because I found out I have her ability." A curling blue flame shot out from her skin.

Luke jumped back in surprise.

Rae stared almost hypnotically at the fire as she slowly coaxed it up her arm and across her body. "Fire can't hurt me. So I figured fire couldn't hurt her as well. And since she was said to have died in a fire...I thought she couldn't really be dead." A few seconds passed, and when Luke didn't say anything, she looked up to see him staring at her in fright.

He caught her looking and tried to force a strained smile. "Okay. So fire can't hurt you..." His voice trailed off as he stared at the flames coming up from her skin. "Rae? Do you mind putting it out anyway?!" he suddenly exclaimed. "You see, not only is my apartment *not* fireproof, but I'm working really hard to resist the urge to cover you in a blanket."

In spite of everything that had just transpired, Rae surprised herself with a sudden giggle. "Stop, drop, and roll, huh?"

"It's not funny," Luke tried to snap, but he couldn't stop the corners of his mouth from rising. "Just...put it out, okay?"

"Fine." Rae obeyed and the fire vanished in a poof of smoke.

Luke shook his head and offered her a hand up. "You never cease to amaze me, Kerrigan."

"I like to keep people guessing." She tried to be casual, but her voice grew soft and sad as she looked again at the blank screen.

"Hey," Luke distracted her, guessing her thoughts, "the video might not have specifically said your mom was alive, but it sure didn't say she was dead either. If fire really couldn't have killed her, then I'd guess there's definitely more to the story than you've always been told."

Rae forced herself to nod and tried to take comfort in his words.

"There was a calendar mounted on the wall behind her," Luke continued, "said the date was March eight. This evidence box didn't get put together and filed on its own. Let me check some security cameras around the area. Maybe, with any luck, I can stumble onto something that we can use to help you find her." He tilted up Rae's chin with two fingers and smiled coaxingly. "You can't give up now, Rae. There's still a chance."

Rae pulled in a shaky breath and smiled back. He was right. There was still a chance.

A small chance.

A chance teetering at the end of a dead-end trail which had left her with a broken VCR and no more clues.

But a chance nonetheless.

"Thanks, Luke." She shut the box and slipped the papers into her coat. "I should probably get back to my friends." She checked her watch. "It's coming up on an hour. I'm pretty sure they've worried themselves into a fright."

"No problem." Luke grabbed his jacket and held open the front door. "I'll walk you."

As she breezed past him onto the walkway and they started down the cobblestone path, she felt that stabbing guilt once again. Luke had risked everything to help her, and in return, she'd smoked up his house, drank the last of his coffee, and broken his VCR. Now, to top it all off, he was willingly escorting her back to where Devon was waiting.

She snuck a peek at him from the corner of her eye. If she hadn't known what had just happened back at the house and where they were going, she might have thought this was just a good-looking guy on a late-night stroll with his girlfriend.

He smiled at her when he saw her looking, but visibly resisted the urge to put his arm around her shoulder—didn't want to get her in trouble with Devon when they got back into view.

How could he be *such* a good guy? What on earth had she done to deserve him? He deserved better, she decided abruptly. He deserved someone who would care for him with as much reckless abandon as he cared for her.

"What are you staring at?"

His question pulled her out of her trance, and she flushed guiltily and dropped her eyes to the wet pavement. "You," she said simply. "You're one of the best guys I know."

With her heightened senses, she literally heard his heart skip a beat in his chest. For a minute, his eyes lit up with a thousand hopeful possibilities, but then they cooled and his face fell.

"But not the best guy," he mumbled softly.

She gulped. *Devon.* It seemed that there was no avoiding him. One way or another, he was her inevitability. It seemed pointless to fight it anymore. She'd said the very words to Molly earlier this evening, and even walking beside this handsome, wonderful man, they rang true.

The heart wants what it wants.

She bit her lip as her voice got as soft as his. "Not the best guy for *me*." She stressed the last word, and although he stiffened beside her, she reached out and caught his hand. "But if I'm being really honest, Luke," her eyes shone in the darkness, "I almost wish you were."

Before he could say anything in reply, they rounded the corner. Molly and Devon stood on the street waiting for them. Devon's eyes immediately fixed on their joined hands and his face hardened. But for the moment, Rae had more pressing problems to deal with. The door to the pub had opened just over Molly's shoulder, and two more people walked out into the night.

The two people, in that particular moment, Rae least wanted to see.

"Good evening, Miss Kerrigan," Carter called as he came to stand beside Devon, Jennifer right at his side. "It seems you have a bit of explaining to do."

"You have got to be kidding me," Rae muttered to herself. The papers she'd taken from her mother's box pressed hard again her chest and she shifted protectively. At least for the time being, they were going to stay her little secret. She locked the video she'd seen firmly behind a door in her memory so Carter wouldn't be able to sneak his way into her memories.

"Well," Luke started backing away, "I guess I'll leave you to it."

Rae lowered her voice so as not to be heard. "You're not going to—"

"Stay and have a secret meeting with the Privy Council in the dead of night?" He raised his eyebrows as he finished her thought. "No, don't think so. I'm going to head back home and salvage whatever's left of my entertainment system. But Rae," his voice became suddenly serious, "I am going to check that security footage we talked about."

Rae's eyes welled with tears but she simply nodded, unable to show her intense gratitude in present company.

With a sarcastic eye roll, Luke gave her a brief, one-armed hug goodbye. But before he left, he glanced back at the four people waiting across the street. "Rae," he called softly, "ask yourself how they found you tonight. Somebody had to have told them what was going on." His eyes swept over Molly and landed on Devon. "I think your mom was asking the right question: who can you trust?"

Across the street, Devon's hands curled into fists and Rae knew he'd heard Luke.

"Thanks Luke," she said sincerely, "for everything."

"Believe it or not, I don't have all night, Miss Kerrigan," Carter called impatiently. "Get over here *now*."

With a parting wave, Rae dodged a taxi and crossed the street to the curb where they were standing. Hovering in the shadow of the two adults, Molly shifted nervously but Devon stood completely on edge. *He looks... guilty*. He kept glancing between Rae and Carter like he was waiting for an actual explosion.

In light of the present situation, Rae could understand his unease.

Not only had they disobeyed a direct order and walked away from a mission, but it was a mission involving the future Queen of England. The punishment for such an action was sure to be severe, and for a moment, Rae wondered with detached curiosity what it might be. It wasn't like they were in school anymore. This was a legitimate job. An adult job—although many of its employees were technically still minors. What could they actually *do* to reprimand her? A slap on the wrist? Suspension? A permanent mark in her file?

Rae smiled to herself as she thought about the look on Luke's face when that information somehow floated across his desk. 'Rae Kerrigan docked ten points for missing curfew while in London on mission.' At least it would serve to lighten his day.

"I'm sorry, Kerrigan," Carter scowled, "is something funny?"

The smile slipped right off Rae's face as she pulled herself back to the moment. Considering the fact that she'd just seen and heard her mother for the first time in over ten years, she felt a little distracted and not quite in the mood to deal with Carter and his uptight rules.

"Not at all, sir." She smiled politely and gestured to the pub sign above their heads. "So what brings you to the Second Sister? I hear their wings are delicious. Not sure they serve them this late."

"Rae!" Devon growled under his breath. She glanced his way and saw Jennifer staring at her with a look of intense exasperation. Molly was standing directly behind her and mouthed a desperate, 'what're you doing?!' behind her head.

Rae sighed. "I'm sorry, sir. It's just been a very long night."

And it had. It was hard to imagine that only about twelve hours ago, she was sitting in a spa with the future queen and getting her hair done to go to a ball. So many things had happened since then. She'd been attacked, kidnapped, drugged, rescued, healed, seen one of her dear friends lose her memory, rekindled a romance with the love of her life, and watched a secret videotape made by her possibly dead mother. She needed to sleep.

"I'll say," Molly interjected hopefully. "Probably best if we all go back and get some rest—"

"Not so fast," Carter cut her off. "You see, Miss Kerrigan, I'm a little puzzled as to what you're doing here when I specifically told you to return to Heath Hall and stay there until morning."

"Well..." Rae's mind scrambled to come up with something plausible, "You see, I—"

"It's no use," Devon interrupted her, stepping forward. "I'm sorry, Rae, but I told him."

Rae's heart froze in her chest. He what?! *What the hell did you tell him?* She shot the thought to Devon using Maria's tatù ability.

She'd just closed a door forever with Luke because this traitor was supposed to be the love of her life, and now here he was, trading her in for the sake of his beloved Privy Council. Her eyes narrowed as she glared at him. This time, she wouldn't be so forgiving.

"I told him about the interview."

Rae's crashing anger came to a sudden halt as she froze. *The interview...?* Her heart began tentatively beating again as she went out on a limb and tried to play along.

"Well, I wish you hadn't." Hopefully that fit the narrative.

Devon shrugged apologetically. "I had no choice. I told Carter that if the Privy Council doesn't want to lose you when your contract expires next year to a university, they were going to have to step up their game."

Molly jumped in, eager to help and surprisingly believable. "I just can't believe the student liaison was willing to meet with you and answer your questions so late. Or should I say so early? Really nice of him."

"Yeah, well I told you," Rae relaxed slightly, slipping into the role, "he's a friend." She turned to Carter. "Sorry for breaking your curfew. I didn't really have a choice. You want me working tomorrow and I don't know how much longer I'll be in London. It was an awkward position to be in. I didn't want to seem ungrateful to you, or the PCs, for everything you've done for me, I just wanted to see what other options there were. I think it's what my mother would have wanted." She directed this last part towards Jennifer and stared right in her eyes, hoping she would understand.

It was difficult to say if she got the message, her face was so impassive, but as she shifted her weight and folded her arms over her chest, Rae could have sworn she saw her wink.

"Why don't we go inside?" Jennifer suggested. "We shouldn't be talking about this out here on the street. Never know who could be listening in."

"Wait a minute." Carter held up his hand in frustration. "You expect me to believe that you were out here tonight meeting with a college counselor? Do you think I'm an idiot?"

"No," Rae said carefully, "I think you're a busy man running a secret organization that has eyes and ears everywhere. Why else do you think I tried to do it this way? I haven't made any sort of decision as to next year yet, and I didn't want to have to talk about it before I was ready."

Carter stared right into her eyes; he seemed to be testing her. For a split second, Rae was terrified he'd touch her skin and somehow see some of her memories of the last few hours.

Instead, he turned to Devon. "Wardell," his voice was hard, "do you swear to me this is the truth?"

A brief shadow crossed over Devon's face, but the next second it was clear.

"It's the truth. Rae went out here tonight to meet a friend and discuss university."

Carter folded his arms across his chest and stood in front of him, toe to toe. "I want your word, Devon. You know how much is riding on this. Both the future of the royal family and your entire career is at stake. I want you to give me your word."

Time seemed to stop in the brief silence that followed. Well this was it, wasn't it? The ultimate test. Rae or the Privy Council. It was a choice she had never wanted Devon to have to make. Partially because she was half-afraid of what he would decide. He had left her once—granted he said that was so she could come into her powers and learn to protect herself—but there were other reasons as well. He believed in the power of the Privy Council, the principles behind it. He risked his life for them on a daily basis, and most of all, he respected their rules. It was his damn rule-following that had come between them many, many times before. Now here it was, all the cards were being laid out on the table. But what Devon was going to choose, Rae had no idea.

She was almost afraid to make eye contact, but she couldn't help but look. Even with Carter facing him in such an aggressive manner, Devon looked calm. His breathing was shallow, but steady, and when he spoke, his voice was sure. "I give you my word, sir. Rae didn't do anything wrong."

Rae felt like she'd been given an electric jolt to the heart. She tried to catch his eye, but he was staring straight back at Carter—his face, an open book.

It was almost impressive, how well he could lie. Almost a little scary.

"Very well." With Devon declaring it so bluntly, Carter appeared satisfied. "However, you're wrong about one thing, Mr. Wardell. Miss Kerrigan certainly did do something wrong. Whatever her reasons were, she was ordered to stay in tonight and she is in direct violation of that order."

Rae saw where he planned to go with this and quickly intervened. "Molly and Devon both told me not to go," she said quickly. "They're only out here because they were trying to talk me out of it and bring me back."

Carter held up his hand to silence her. "What's done is done. You three are going back to Heath Hall this instant to get some sleep before waking up at seven a.m. to debrief." He checked his watch. "That's just about five hours from now. I suggest you hurry back."

No formal censure?! They didn't need to be told twice.

"Yes, sir," Devon said obediently, and quickly hailed down a cab. He and the girls slid inside, and before they knew it, they were racing back down the streets of London, leaving two adults standing on the curb locked in hushed discussion.

"What do you think they're talking about?" Molly asked. Her eye had developed a strange twitch that Rae had never seen before and Rae frowned before answering.

"I've no idea." She eyed Devon tentatively. "Maybe they were discussing what incentives they can offer me to keep me from going back to school?"

He still wouldn't look at her. He just stared out the window, avoiding eye contact.

"Or maybe they were actually going there for the wings," she said a little louder. "After all, why else would they have come?"

Molly's eyes grew wide and twitched again as she realized her friend's implication. "Rae, I didn't say a thing! I didn't tell anybody where we were going tonight!"

"It's not you Molls, don't worry," Devon said, keeping his eyes fixed on the window. "She's talking about me."

Rae took a steadying breath. She hadn't planned on bringing it up this quickly, especially in light of Devon's amazing cover for her back with Carter, but the question remained. How did Carter and Jennifer know where to find them?

"Why don't you just ask me?"

She looked up in surprise and saw Devon staring at her from the opposite seat. There was a look of steely determination in his eyes, but it was covering something deeper. A sadness.

Rae bit her lip, but closed her eyes and blurted, "Did you tell them?"

Molly gasped as her eye twitched again.

Devon clenched his jaw. "Did I tell them you were sneaking out, then swear on my reputation that you'd just gone to see a university counselor?"

When he phrased it like that, it didn't make much sense. Only, who else could it be? Rae would bet her life it wasn't Molly, and Devon was literally the only other person who knew.

"I'm just trying to figure out how they knew where to look for me," she said quietly.

"And I'm just telling you, it wasn't me!"

Molly twitched again in between them, and for a minute, the conversation paused.

"What is going *on* with you?" Rae asked in exasperation. "Why do you keep doing that?"

"Sorry," Molly gulped and smoothed down her static-ridden hair. "I've been giving myself little shocks to help me stay awake."

There was a beat of silence, before the cab was filled with sudden laughter. Hysterical laugher. The kind indicative of a bigger problem, but perfect in the moment to soothe raw nerves.

Molly glared between Rae and Devon as they collapsed on their seats, clinging to the leather as they tried to pull themselves together.

"What?!" she demanded. "It's almost three in the morning, I've been up since five."

"This whole time?" Devon asked incredulously. The cab slowed down as it pulled into the long drive of Heath Hall. "You've been giving yourself shock therapy this whole time?"

"Well, ever since Carter and Jennifer walked into the pub," Molly said defensively. "I thought it would look unprofessional if I fell asleep in my cappuccino."

Rae and Devon began snickering again, and Molly fumed as she pulled open her door and stomped up the front steps.

"Laugh it up you two. I'm not the one who has to debrief at seven in the morning. In the meantime, I hope you guys have fun tonight...working through your major issues."

With that, she stomped upstairs to her room as the sound of Rae and Devon's laughter faded suddenly in the cold night.

Chapter 7

The silence that followed Molly's departure was almost as loud as the laughter a second before. The taxi driver rotated slowly in his seat and raised his eyebrows knowingly, flashing both Devon and Rae an accusatory look. A faint blush appeared high on Devon's cheekbones as he thrust a wad of bills into the man's hands and muttered, "Keep the change."

Neither he nor Rae really looked at each other as they walked in silence up the old stone steps and made their way down the ornate hallway to their room. When Devon pulled open the door, a mixed aroma of citrus cleaning supplies and fresh roses struck them both at the same time. Devon headed for the kitchen to see if the staff had re-stocked the fridge while Rae went to examine an expensive-looking bouquet of wine red roses sitting in a vase on the coffee table.

Up close, the fragrance was pleasantly overpowering and Rae shut her eyes, drawing in a deep breath before picking up the attached card. It was a thick stock paper, written in a neat, formal hand:

To our new favorite couple,

We hope you enjoy the flowers as a token of our sincere appreciation for your continued support and companionship. It means the world to us to have the two of you by our side in this exciting time. We really don't know how we would have managed at the ball tonight without you—it just wouldn't have been the same. Thank goodness for Spanish class, right? Otherwise, we'd never have met!

With affection and thanks,
Philip and Sarah

HRH

Rae couldn't help but smile to herself after reading the last line. So she'd told him. Sarah had told Philip their big secret. Despite the monumental gravity of that decision, Rae was hardly surprised. She'd almost figured their conversation had been headed that way after Philip said he'd be willing to abdicate the thrown to keep his fiancé safe. Another monumental decision. But it was par for the course. These people were royals, through and through. They didn't do anything halfway.

It must be nice, Rae thought absently, stroking the petals of a rose. *Having a person who'd be willing to give up their entire life for you.* Some mugs rattled in the kitchen and she looked up to see Devon making a pot of coffee, still carefully avoiding her gaze.

What was she talking about?! Wasn't that exactly what Devon had just done for her? He'd risked his job and his reputation, all to cover up for her lie. And what had she done in return? She'd accused him of betraying her.

"Those from your boyfriend?" Devon asked softly from the kitchen, staring down with determination at the mugs. "Or should I say, your college counselor?" He tried for a smile, but he looked so sad Rae's heart broke.

"They're not from him. And he's not my boyfriend." She waved the card in the air and tried to lighten the mood. "It's actually from Sarah and Philip, thanking us for accompanying them to the ball. Apparently, it wouldn't have been the same without us."

Even Devon had to smile at that one. "Yeah, I bet." He carried over two steaming mugs and set one down on the table before her. "Yours is hot chocolate," he quickly assured her. "I know you don't like to drink coffee after nine..."

For whatever reason, those words struck them both instantly sad. Maybe it was the fact that despite their time apart, Devon still remembered every little detail. Maybe it was the fact that they hadn't spent casual time together in so long.

For what seemed like an eternity, the two of them stared down into their mugs, listening to the second hand tick away on the kitchen clock. Then, with no warning, they looked up at the same time. Both in a sudden rush to speak.

"Look Devon, I'm really sorry—"

"You still don't trust me!"

Rae was taken aback by the anger and passion in his voice. She had been trying to apologize, not start a huge argument. But from the looks of things, Molly was probably right. If they ever wanted to move forward, they were going to have to air out these issues, once and for all.

For the last two years, he's been perfectly positioned to gain your trust.

Luke's words echoed in her brain, but she pushed them aside. If she was being really honest with herself, this had nothing to do with the last two years. The root of their problem, and all Rae's newfound defensiveness, was much more specific.

"I risked my job to save you just now," Devon continued when she didn't say anything. "I gave Carter my word—and I'm sure he's going to have all night to pick it apart and he's going to grill us tomorrow in the morning debriefing. I risked everything for you Rae." He struggled to keep his voice steady. "And after all this time, you still don't trust me?!"

"That's the problem, Devon!" Rae finally exploded. "I did trust you! I trusted you with everything—with my very heart— and you left me!"

Devon's face paled. "We went over this," he murmured. "I did it to keep you safe."

"But that's bullshit!" she exclaimed. "And it doesn't change the fact that it happened. You *left*!"

"Well what the hell can I do about that now? How can I get us past this?"

Rae threw up her hands. "I don't know," she answered sincerely. "Maybe it just has to fix itself in time?"

She perched on the edge of the coffee table and tried to calm down, breathing in slowly and inhaling the airy scent of roses. Yelling wasn't going to help things along. She just had to be level-headed and tell the truth. It was the only way to move forward.

"Devon, I can't shake the feeling that the second things get rough, you could just disappear on me again. And what's worse, you wouldn't ever tell me why. You'd just do it 'for my own good' or something. I need to be with someone who's going to treat me like a partner—an equal. Someone that's going to stick by me in thick or thin."

Rae couldn't believe the words coming out of her mouth. She wasn't talking life or death here, she wasn't thinking thirty years ahead. But she was willing to fully commit to him. To commit herself to the hazards and happiness of being in love. To give him her heart again—no matter how scary. She just didn't know if he was willing to do the same.

Be it the Privy Council, the rules about tatùs never mixing, the disapproval of his father, or even these random 'for Rae's own good' things he came up with on his own.

Sometimes it felt like they were sitting on top of a tinder box playing with matches. She never knew which one of them could set the whole thing aflame.

"I will always, *always* be there for you." The sincerity on his face was impossible to ignore, but at the same time, it looked like there was a battle raging on beneath the surface. A battle between how he'd lived his whole life, and the life he wanted to have.

Rae smiled sadly. "I really want to believe you. I know, in a lot of ways, it's easier for me. I didn't grow up with these rules the way you did." She gave a wry laugh. "I don't even have a family to disapprove. But what I am an expert in, is loss. I don't want to lose you, Devon. I couldn't take it. You're obsessed with protecting me?" She raised her eyebrows. "Well, I have to protect me too. Whether it's from crazy half-brothers...or just from getting my heart broken all over again."

The two of them stared at each other for another minute before Rae slowly got to her feet. "I'm going to bed," she said softly. "Only have a few hours before we have to get up for the debriefing." As she walked off to her room, her fingers grazed lightly across his shoulder. "Thanks for the hot chocolate." She got all the way to her door before she heard him answer her quietly, still sitting in the dark.

"Any time."

It felt like the second Rae closed her eyes, they snapped open again to the frantic buzzing of her alarm. In the next room over, she could hear Devon stirring as well. With an exhausted groan, she pressed the pillow over her face and thought jealously of Molly, still sleeping away upstairs.

Well, this debriefing had to start sooner or later. Best to get it over with.

Without Molly there to dictate her clothing, she dressed simply. An airy, light blue blouse with fitted white slacks. She pulled up her curls into a loose half-ponytail and opted for only a swipe of mascara and some light pink lip gloss. When she was finished, she pulled back for a cursory glance in the mirror.

It came together rather nicely, she thought. It didn't have Molly's glamour and flash, but it was sleek and stylish. A bit understated, but feminine and soft. It was Rae.

She paired it with some professional-looking pumps and rushed out to the kitchen to find Devon already waiting there with coffee.

This time, he didn't avoid her gaze. Instead, he looked straight into her eyes as he flashed his dimples at her. "Good morning," he said brightly.

She took the coffee hesitantly, waiting for the other shoe to drop. After last night, she thought that their relationship would be as strained as ever, but Devon was looking pleased and put together. There was a steadiness about him that hadn't been there for a long time. It was almost as if, Rae didn't know what word to put to it, he was...at peace?

"Morning," she answered cautiously. Her voice was scratchy and every muscle in her body was sore from lack of sleep. "You sure look...awake." After her three hours of sleep, the concept of 'awake' was foreign to her.

Devon laughed cheerfully, the sound echoed in the little room. "Yeah well, we have to start the day out right, don't we?"

Rae raised her eyebrows as she took a scalding sip. "If that's true, I'm not sure a crack of dawn debriefing with Carter is the way to go."

"We'll just tell him what happened at the ball," Devon said simply. He pulled out an apple and quickly cut it into slices, tipping a few onto a plate before sliding it her way. "We're heroes, after all. Or at least, you are." He looked suddenly proud. "You found the future queen. You risked everything to save her."

"And I got kidnapped and drugged in the process." Rae nibbled the end of an apple. "But I guess everything worked out in the end. Except for Maria." She frowned in sudden concern. In the rush of everything that had happened last night, she had almost forgotten about her poor brainwashed friend. "Is she going to be okay? Is Curtis working on her?"

"I'm sure she's going to be fine." Devon laid a reassuring hand on her arm. The warmth of it sent tingles flying up her skin. "Curtis seemed really confident. I'm sure he can reverse the process."

Rae didn't want to ask, but she had to. "And when Carter asks us about last night?" She glanced up nervously at Devon's face, but found that he was staring steadily back at her.

"Whatever happens, we'll face it together." He reached down and squeezed her fingers. "I promise. No matter what."

With a confident wink, he turned back to his breakfast, but Rae found herself staring at her now empty hand. What had happened between three and seven in the morning? Last night, Devon looked shaken—rattled to his very core. Today, he was a new man. Bustling around the kitchen and hand-holding and winking? Making solidarity promises? She really didn't know what to make of it.

She was about to ask when a sudden buzzing on her phone caught her attention. Who on earth would be texting at seven in the morning? Perhaps when she signed on with the Privy Council she should have made things clear—she was not a morning person. She downed the rest of her coffee in a steaming gulp and flicked on the screen. It was a text from Luke.

Rae glanced automatically at Devon, but he was breezing around the living room, looking for his jacket and shoes. Perfect. She reached for his coffee and scanned the message.

Rae. Don't have much time to talk. Never know who could be watching. Stayed up all night looking through surveillance feeds and you're not going to believe what I found. We need to meet as soon as possible. Where are you?

What the hell?! She frowned at the screen and began typing a quick reply.

"Rae, have you seen my coffee?" Devon called from the living room.

"No, uh, you must not have poured any yet." She took another swig and hit send.

I don't have much time either, about to go into a debriefing. I'm at a place called Heath Hall on the outskirts of London. But it's like PC headquarters and I don't think you can come here. I'd go to you, but they're watching me pretty carefully after I snuck out last night.

"Didn't pour any yet, huh?" Devon chuckled and kissed her on the tip of the nose. "Very funny, you little thief. Now come on, we don't want to keep Carter waiting."

Rae caught her breath as he headed out the door. She didn't know if she would ever get used to him casually kissing her again.

"Rae! Come on!"

She shook her head and snapped back to the present. "Coming!" She snatched up her coat and rushed to follow him, but as she was going, her phone buzzed again in her hand.

Doesn't matter whose headquarters it is. I'm coming. See you soon.

Her heart skipped a beat. Great. If there was one thing that could ruin Devon's inexplicable good mood and get her into even more trouble with Carter, it was a visit from her mysterious college counselor. But under the initial layer of stress, her head spun in a million different directions.

What on earth was so important that Luke was willing to walk into enemy headquarters?

What had he seen?!

She barely had time to contemplate this before she and Devon were out the door, rushing to the spacious guest house at the other side of the property. They raced across the wide lawns, dodging the freezing arch of the morning sprinklers.

"Carter planned it like this," Rae muttered as she put on a sudden burst of speed to avoid getting sprayed. "He knew exactly when these damn things would come on."

Much to her surprise, Devon just laughed and pulled her gently along. "It's highly unlikely, but I wouldn't totally rule it out. Hey, nothing like a morning shower, right?"

Rae chuckled in spite of herself. "What did you take? Happy pills or something?"

"Just glad to be in London on a beautiful morning with my gorgeous...Rae." He smiled and she wondered how he would have liked to have finished that sentence. "Come on, I can see Carter is already inside."

They rushed in to see not just Carter, but Jennifer sitting on two of the three guest house sofas. They were set up to face each other, making a broken triangle, leaving Rae and Devon to sit on the third one together. While it looked innocuous enough by itself, once the two of them sat down, Rae thought the formation made the whole thing feel suspiciously like an interrogation.

"Good morning," Carter began briskly, "I hope you both slept well."

"Fine," Rae said wryly, flicking a few water drops from her fingers.

Carter smiled. "Good, then let's not waste time."

"Yes, sir." Devon leaned forward with his elbows on his knees. Rae was happy to let him take the lead. He had done these debriefings many times before. "We arrived at the location of the ball at precisely nineteen hundred hours, just ahead of Maria and Curtis. At the time, our risk assessment was—"

"What really happened last night?" Carter interrupted.

On her sofa, Jennifer leaned forward intently but kept quiet.

Devon looked confused. "I was just trying to tell you, sir."

"Not at the ball," Carter said. "I already know what happened at the ball, and I must say, the two of you did very well considering the circumstances. I'm talking about afterwards." His eyes fixed on Rae. "Where did you go? And don't say that it was to meet with a counselor. I mean for Pete's sake, kids, we teach you how to lie."

Rae's blood rose to a boil. Kids? Really? *No.* He wasn't allowed to go back and forth that easily. Either they were kids— to be taught and given a curfew. Or they were adults. Put into the line of fire but trusted and allowed to make decisions on their own. He didn't get to have it both ways.

"I'm sorry, *sir*," her eyes narrowed, "I don't know exactly what you're insinuating."

"Rae." Jennifer only said one word, but it carried a weight and a warning. She was to watch herself. Rae's eyes fell obediently to her lap, and Devon took over.

"Sir, I apologize for the timing, but since we were in London with nothing to do for a few hours, Rae took the opportunity to—"

"Wardell, that's enough!" For whatever reason, Carter seemed especially upset with Devon. Like Devon's was a double betrayal. "I've given your story to the rest of the Privy Council and they don't believe it any more than we do." He pulled himself up to his full height. "You two are officially on probation, pending further investigation."

"*What*?!" Rae and Devon exploded at the same time.

"Sir, you can't do that!"

"Listen Carter, we did exactly what we were supposed to do. We saved the future queen just like you wanted, at great personal risk I might add, and then—"

Carter stood up. "Then you lied to me!" He was visibly struggling to control his temper. "You disobeyed a direct order, looked me in the eye, and lied about it. This is an organization built upon trust and respect. It is a privilege to work for." He glared at them both, standing in the center of the floor between the sofas. "I thought you, at least, understood that Mr. Wardell. I must have been mistaken."

Devon flushed to the roots of his hair and his face fell.

Rae, however, was incensed. "Okay, so the next time we take off after we've *successfully completed our mission*, we'll be sure to let you guys know where we're going. You know," she knew she was crossing a line, but couldn't find it in herself to care, "maybe you guys can just inject us with those little microchips they put in dogs. That way, the next time we go out, you can just track us by following the little flashing dot!"

"I don't think you understand the gravity of what's going on here, young lady," Carter growled. "You two are under fire. Under scrutiny and on probation. To be separated from the rest of the Council until we can determine what's really going on and whether or not we can trust—"

"*I was going to find my mom!*" Rae's ears rang in the deafening silence that followed as she got to her feet and squared off in front of Carter.

The words had a profound effect on every person in the room. Devon dropped his face into his hands, while Jennifer had gone very still, watching Rae's every move with eyes like a hawk's. But it was Carter whose reaction was the strangest. It was like he was melting. His shoulders sagged and his eyes filled with a mix of pity and horror.

"Is that what you wanted to hear?" Rae trembled with rage. "Is that the information your precious Privy Council so badly wants to know? I know she's out there. She left me a box of clues that I went to collect last night. This whole time I've just—" The sudden burst of passion and energy seemed to have taken all the wind from Rae's sails, and she finished in a small, defeated sounding voice. "I've just been trying to find her."

No one said a word afterwards. For a very, very long time. A jet from the sprinklers shot up against the window, making them all jump, but it was dead quiet inside the room.

Until...a soft but determined voice broke the silence.

"I'll help you." In a flash, Jennifer was on her feet, standing in between Rae and Carter in the center of the room. "I'll help you find Bethany. She was my friend. There's no way in hell I'm letting you do this alone."

Rae's eyes welled up with grateful tears, but before she could speak, a heart-wrenching wail shook the walls of the little house. She turned her eyes to Carter instead, stunned and bewildered.

"There is no *finding* Bethany, because there *is* no Bethany!" he shouted. Silent tears slipped unnoticed down his neck, wetting the top of his starched collar. "Don't you dare encourage her, Jennifer! Don't you dare get her hopes up! Bethany's dead!"

"You don't know that—"

Rae grabbed his arm, but all at once, the world around her disappeared. Her body had instinctively switched tatùs, using

Carter's own tatù against him, showing her what she most needed to see.

Rae gasped aloud as all at once, a million different images rushed through her head. She was seeing her mom, but from a million different vantage points. Her mom wowing everyone with her incredible talent in the Oratory. Her mom walking across the grass as the sun caught in her dark hair. Her mom laughing with friends at the same pub Rae and her friends frequented in town.

All through the eyes...of Carter.

Rae jumped back as if she'd been shocked. Her eyes snapped open and she stared at Carter in astonishment. All this time, it had been right under her nose.

"You're in love with my mom!"

Chapter 8

"How dare you!" Carter roared. "Get the hell out of my head!"

Rae stumbled backwards and half fell into Devon's arms, stunned by both the force of the memory and Carter's explosive anger.

"Rae," Devon whispered into her ear, "what's going on?"

She couldn't answer him. She couldn't even bring herself to be properly afraid of Carter. She was too busy trying to recollect the image of her young mother. Beth couldn't have been much older than Rae's age now. Their resemblance was extraordinary! People had told her that before, but she'd never realized how similar they were. They could pass as twins and no one would have said a thing – except her mom would be way older now.

As she remembered the sun glinting off her mother's raven hair, she took one of her own curls absently between her fingers. They even had the same hair. She'd always thought it was her dad's hair, like Kraigan. Maybe it was a bit of both.

"Are you even listening to me?!" Carter raged on.

"You were in love with her," Rae repeated, softer than before. She had tuned out for a moment, but she looked up at him now as if realizing the implications of it for the first time. "Why didn't you tell me? Did she even know?"

It seemed as though the one thing Carter wasn't prepared for was quiet curiosity. His attacks crumbled and he simply stared at Rae with hollow, burning eyes. After a long, awkward minute, it was actually Jennifer who stepped forward.

"That was a long time ago," she murmured in a surprisingly gentle voice. "Let's just focus on the present, shall we? You said you went to London to recover a box..." All at once, she straightened and became hyper-alert, reminding Rae of the leopard waiting just below. "Where's the box now? Did you open it?"

Rae shook her head distractedly. "No, I'd like to stay on this for a minute." She folded her arms over her chest and fixed Carter in a critical gaze. "What happened between you and my mom?"

Carter managed to calm down, but he still had visibly little control of himself. "Nothing." It came out as almost a whisper. "She was with Simon. I admired her from afar. Nothing ever happened. The two of them were in love. There was never room for anyone else. And it is none of your business."

"Why not? You've used your tatù on me. Why would I not have the right to use it back?" She hadn't meant to use it, her body had simply flipped and Carter had obviously not been prepared any more than she had.

For whatever reason, Jennifer flashed him a pained expression and started abruptly pacing in the back of the room.

Rae stared at her, as if mesmerized by the human pendulum. Hadn't she thought Jennifer was in love with Carter and he had no idea? These tatùs sure lived complicated lives.

Devon and Rae stared between them, completely dumbfounded.

"Leave it to you, Rae," Devon murmured into her ear. "Weirdest debriefing. Ever."

She was still in his arms, and when he spoke, a whole other wave of implication clicked into place. She turned back to Carter. "And you see fit to put *us* on probation?" She pointed a shaking finger at him as her blood boiled in rage. "Here you're punishing me for breaking one of your precious curfew rules, and you fell in love with another tatù!"

"You're one to talk!" Carter spat. "Look at the two of you!"

Devon quickly released Rae from his arms, but it was too late. The damage had already been done. "Sir, it's nothing—"

"He's in love with you!" Carter threw up his hands in exasperation. "No matter how many times I tried to separate the two of you. How many missions I sent him on just to keep him away. It didn't matter. He's head over heels in love with you, and I honestly think the only person who can't see it, Miss Kerrigan, is you."

Rae's heart froze in her chest and she sensed, rather than felt, Devon stiffen beside her. However, Carter wasn't finished. He ignored the stricken looks on their faces and kept right on going.

"And whether you love him back...?" He laughed derisively. "Well Rae, your parents' cautionary tale be damned. The only thing more obvious than whether Devon loves you is how much you love him back. Even when I tried to distract you by pairing you up with Julian, you held strong. Everyone knows. The students, the faculty. You tried to deny it and hide it, but you can't miss a fire when it's burning right in front of you."

Jennifer swept forward and put a cautioning hand on Carter's shoulder. "Carter, please, you've made your point. I think what everybody needs now is to calm down and get back to—"

Carter flicked her hand off. "Tell me, Mr. Wardell," he sneered in Devon's face, "how long did you think you could keep it a secret? From your father? From the Council? You're a smart boy, so tell me. How long did you think you could hide the fact you'd fallen in love with one of our own?"

Devon's face was a warzone of different emotions, but when he spoke, his voice came out restrained and calm. "I've *no idea* what you're talking about. I think Jennifer's right, you're obviously unwell." The words were cold as ice. "Perhaps you need to take some time to collect yourself and we'll finish the debriefing later."

Carter laughed and the sound of it sent chills up Rae's spine. She had never seen him so unhinged. Not even with Lanford or Kraigan. Even at the worst of times, he'd always managed to keep it together, to act like he had a purpose. But now? He seemed completely deranged. Pacing around in frantic circles, running his fingers repeatedly through his hair. From the minute Rae said Beth's name, it was like he didn't realize he still had tears running down his face.

"Really?" Carter laughed again. "You're going to deny it? You're going to sit there in front of me like the Privy Council's golden boy and claim you've no feelings for this girl?"

What the hell is going on? Why is he acting like this?

Rae sent the message telepathically to Jennifer and waited anxiously for a reply. There was an almost imperceptible pause in her mentor's pacing and she shot Rae a look. A look that revealed nothing, but warned her to keep quiet.

Devon ground his teeth together and struggled to keep himself in check. "Maybe...maybe I did once. When she first got to Guilder, I admit, I was attracted to her. Lanford paired us up. He forced me to spend time with her. I was a kid, who wouldn't have a crush on the pretty new girl?" He shook his head and stared at Carter with honest, open eyes. "That was years ago and I never did a thing about it. I've moved on. I've dated other people."

That chilling laugh stopped him dead in his tracks. "The fact that you would even try to deny it is hilarious." Carter's eyes gleamed. "After all the time we've spent together? After all the times I've seen your memories?"

It was like the air in the room dropped ten degrees. Devon's lips parted like he was going to say something, but instead he just stared at Carter in horrified silence. His face pale with shock. "You didn't..."

Carter grinned triumphantly. "Every handshake, every smile. Every time I clapped you on the shoulder when you came back from a mission. I *know* how you feel, Devon. I saw it."

"You used your tatù on me," Devon's voice rose in anger, "without my permission?!"

It was an unspoken rule in the tatù community. As basic as 'not raising a hand against your neighbor.' You *never* used your tatù on someone else without first informing them you were going to do so. It was why Rae was so careful about whose talents she got to absorb. Sure kids played around and pranked each other back at Guilder, but never in a serious way. Not like this. This was low and dirty. It was unforgivable.

"Every day," Carter said softly. It was like the weight of the confession had subdued him. "I saw Rae how you see her, I saw her through your eyes. I haven't felt a love like that since..." He stopped short at the look on Devon's face.

For a wild second, Rae thought Devon might actually leap across the room and beat Carter to death.

He crossed the floor in a blur of speed, but instead of striking Carter, he just stood there. Then he did the last thing Rae ever expected. He rolled up his sleeve and extended his arm. "Then look again."

Carter hesitated but Devon's eyes flashed as he insisted.

"Look again, Carter. And tell me what you see."

After a heavy pause, Carter slowly, almost reluctantly, reached out and wrapped his fingers around Devon's arm by his elbow. Both Jennifer and Rae watched with wide eyes as the tatù went into effect. Both men flinched, almost as if they'd been startled by something, then they locked eyes.

Devon stared at Carter. Carter stared into Devon's thoughts.

Both were unreadable. Both were unmovable.

Then suddenly, Carter's eyes filled with fresh tears. His head snapped up and he stared at Devon like he'd never seen him before, searching his face as he slowly released his arm.

"Now," Devon was barely breathing, "tell me how what you saw is wrong."

You could have heard a pin drop. Rae felt like she was going to explode with unanswered questions, but the two men stared each other down like it was only the two of them in the room. A full minute passed, each second dragging on like hours.

Just as Carter opened his mouth to say something, Devon stormed from the room.

Rae blinked. *What the hell just happened?!*

In the beat of the next second she tore off after him. She didn't care that she was leaving an official meeting without being dismissed. She didn't care she'd left her mentor and her boss in the dust behind her. She had to get to Devon. She needed to find out what all this meant.

As she breezed through the door, she heard Jennifer call, "Rae, we're going to sort this out. We'll send Molly back to Guilder so Carter and I can move in above you. We'll...make this right."

Rae didn't respond. No freakin' way was crazy Carter living above her. She slammed the door behind her and took off across the lawn. Damn it. Sometimes she forgot how fast Devon was. There was no sign of him. Slipping into his own tatù, she put on a rush of speed and darted across the sweeping grass, flying through the door of the main house before coming to an abrupt stop in the living room.

Devon was standing in the middle of the floor, staring out towards the gardens. His back was to her, so she couldn't gauge his mood. She had a pretty damn good idea though.

He didn't move as she came up softly beside him; he didn't even acknowledge her. He just stood there. Unreadable. Unmovable. Exactly how he'd been with Carter just moments before. To be honest, Rae wasn't even sure he'd registered her presence.

"Devon?" She put a tentative hand on his wrist and felt him jump beneath her. "Are you...are you okay?"

"Rae," he answered in reply.

Much to her great surprise, he relaxed his posture and smiled. Without seeming to think about it, he reached out and stroked her hair.

She didn't want to ask, but she had to. She had to know. One way or another. She had to know what it was that Carter saw. Her very future depended on it. "Devon...what happened back there? What did—what did Carter see?"

There was a little pause, like the plunge before the fall, before Devon gave her a small half-smile and tucked a stray lock behind her ear. "Rae, did I ever tell you that when I was growing up I had a dog?"

She blinked. "Um...no. To be perfectly honest, I'm not sure I really care."

He smiled again but continued undeterred. "When I was about five or six, we were living in the countryside outside of London. It was a big old manor house, much too big for just the three of us, and I was lonely. I missed my city friends and my city life. Even at five years old I had high expectations." He chuckled. "Anyway, I asked my father and mother one day if I could get a dog. A companion to play with as I roamed the empty halls and gardens. My mother didn't care much, but my father flat out refused. He hated animals and didn't want to have one on the property. But, as fate would have it, a farmer hit a stray dog on the road outside our house the very next day."

Devon's eyes grew distant as he remembered, while Rae was in a state of frozen anticipation. He had never much talked about his childhood and she was absolutely mesmerized by the story. But at the same time, she had her own story that needed finishing. Couldn't this wait?!

"The poor thing was lame in two legs and had a couple broken ribs," he continued. "Couldn't clean, walk, or feed itself. My father was disgusted. He headed inside to get his hunting rifle to shoot it, but I threw myself in front of it. I begged him to let me keep it, just long enough to nurse it back to health. My mother threw her clout on my side, and eventually, however reluctantly, he agreed. I got to work the very next day.

"First I made a bed for her. I cleaned her off and cooked her what I thought was a suitable 'dog meal' from whatever I found in the kitchen. Then, with my mother's help, I braced her broken ribs. I spent hours every day, sitting with her outside. Sometimes I even read to her." He chuckled again at his boyish silliness. "Days stretched into weeks stretched into months. Eventually, she got strong enough to take care of herself. When my father came home one day and saw her walking around, I was terrified he'd take her away. But he just looked at me, simple as you please, and said, 'Son, I guess she can stay'."

When the story finished, Devon returned his gaze to the window. The same peaceful, unconcerned smile still lingering on his face. Eventually, Rae broke the silence.

"Okay, so," her voice dropped to a whisper, "I'm the dog?"

Devon turned to face her square on. "Carter saw that I'm absolutely in love with you. In a way that doesn't know boundaries or rules. In a way that people write novels and poetry about. You're my every thought. My every concern. And my every hope for the future. All I want is you, Rae. You're my whole life."

Rae's heart was beating so hard she could see it pounding in her chest.

You're my whole life.

It was her fairytale. Her dream. All wrapped up in four neat little words.

But that meant...

"Wait..." she said slowly, "*that's* what Carter saw? The head of the Privy Council?"

Devon chuckled and took her gently by the hands. "I guess I'm not making myself clear. I don't care, Rae. This isn't some passing fancy for me. I want to..." he stared deeply into her eyes, rubbing soft circles on her palms, "I want to spend the rest of my life with you. I tried to fight it." He laughed ruefully. "Lord knows I tried to fight it. But at the Royal Tea Gala, when I thought I'd lost you...I realized I could never live without you. Even if that meant just working alongside you and never admitting my feelings, it would always be you. You're it for me, Rae. I'm done—cashing in all my chips. All I want is a life spent forever with you."

For one of the first times in her life, Rae was utterly speechless. She felt like she was floating off the floor, unable to stay grounded in the face of such euphoria. Everything Devon was saying, all his feelings and hopes for the future, she felt them stirring deep in her own heart. It had always been this way, she realized. She'd just needed him to say it aloud to know it for herself.

They were meant for each other.

There was nothing in the world that could ever change that.

"I..." the dizzy happiness she was feeling was making it hard to speak, "I want that too."

"You do?" Devon almost laughed in relief, bringing their faces together so they were only an inch or two away. "I thought maybe...maybe I'd missed my chance."

Rae shook her head fiercely. "Devon, how could you miss your chance? It's *always* been you. I think...I think I've actually known it from the first moment we met. You're the one for me."

His smile was almost blinding and she shut her eyes for a split second to remember it. This was a moment she would never forget. She knew it in her heart. Years and years down the road, she'd look back and realize this was the moment that everything changed.

Then he kissed her.

She closed her eyes again and vanished, losing herself completely in that kiss. Her hands tangled in his hair as his laced around her lower back, holding her tight against him. In all her life, Rae had never felt more centered, more right. It was quite simply the happiest she had ever been, except it wasn't a kind of happiness she was used to. It was the kind of happiness that filled a part of you that you never knew was missing. The kind of happiness you felt when you finally, after a long journey, came home.

The consequences be damned. They could deal with them tomorrow.

Today, they were in their own little world. Tonight was for them.

Rae hardly even noticed as Devon picked her up and carried her to the bedroom.

This was their fairytale. For however long it lasted.

Chapter 9

There comes a time in every dream, no matter how good or how real, when you have to open your eyes and wake up.

"He's not moving!" Rae shrieked. "Devon, he's barely breathing!"

A steady pool of blood soaked slowly into the plush carpet and she felt the room around her spin. How had this happened? A few hours ago, everything had been perfect...

For the first time in her life, Rae had woken up in the arms of the boy she loved. At first, she'd been afraid to open her eyes, scared that when she did, she'd discover she had made the whole thing up. But there was Devon, smiling back at her in the golden glow of the setting sun.

Strangely enough, it was that moment which stuck with her more than any other. Not to say that the last few hours, locked away in their own little bubble, hadn't been some of the best of her life. It had been everything she'd ever imagined, and she'd imagined quite a lot. But it was that moment after, the moment that let her know it wasn't over. Devon was still there when she woke up. Things were just beginning.

Then the world had come crashing down.

"Call an ambulance!"

"Rae, can you feel his pulse?"

"Call nine-nine-nine!" she shrieked. She remembered what he'd asked and grabbed at a pale wrist. "It's...yeah, it's there. But just barely! It's really faint!" A dry sob caught in her throat as she looked down at the boy lying on the ground beneath her.

Luke.

He lay sprawled out on the floor, blood from a major head wound spilling less generously now through his blond hair and onto the ground beneath. His clothes were disheveled and ripped, his knuckles and hands bruised like he'd put up one hell of a fight.

Rae fell to the ground beside him and tore her cardigan off to stop the bleeding. Guilty, broken tears welled up in her eyes, but she refused to let them fall. Instead, she pressed the sweater firmly to Luke's head and listened as Devon called for help in the background.

"This is Devon Wardell, calling from Heath Hall in London. We've got a man down. Around six foot one, twenty years of age. It appears to be a concussion sustained from a severe head wound. Send back up immediately."

He hung up and Rae met his eyes with a look of wild confusion.

"We don't call nine-nine-nine," he explained, as he rushed to the living room beside her. "Whatever Luke was doing here was apparently not sanctioned by either organization and can't just be explained away to the police. We'll have our own medics transport him to the hospital."

The Privy Council had their own ambulance service full of physicians? She'd never known. Not that it mattered now that she had Charles' tatù.

Wait! She knew the healing tatù could only be used on her, but if she tried, really tried, could it work? Using every bit of focus and determination she had, she placed her free hand on Luke's forehead and shut her eyes. *There has to be a way*, she thought as she steadied her breathing and tried to channel the healing tatù. *There has to be a way to project it onto him.*

"Rae, what're you doing?" Devon wrapped his hand gently around hers and stared down into her panicked face.

"I'm trying to heal him, using Charles' tatù," she gasped with the strain.

Devon frowned. "Is that...can his tatù even do that? I thought it was limited to the carrier."

"I don't know," she wailed, "but if there were ever a time to find out, it would be now!"

Nothing happened. Rae hadn't really believed it would. Luke stayed as cold and quiet as ever beneath her shaking hand.

"It looks like someone ripped this place apart," Devon muttered as he looked around. He had stuffed his own jacket beneath Luke's head to prop him up and was kneeling beside him in a watchful, protective sort of way. "We've only been here a few days and it's just a cover. Everything of value is either back with Curtis or down at headquarters. I wonder what the hell they could have been looking for..."

Rae sucked in a quick breath. It couldn't have been a coincidence. Luke tells her that he found something on a surveillance feed, something that she needs to see, the very day after she meets him in London to recover the contents of the box. This had something to do with her mother, she had no doubt about it. This had something to do with...

"The files!" she screeched, staring wildly around. "My mother's files!"

"It's okay, just calm down." Devon tried to steady her. "Where did you put them?"

Rae tried to think back. "They were in my jacket when we got home last night. Since you and I stayed up a bit and talked, I slipped them out and put them..." Her eyes fell on the ransacked coffee table by the front door. It had been overturned, one leg smashed off, and the center drawer where she had stashed the papers was gone. "I put them in there," she finished, gesturing with her head. "They're gone."

There was an escalating pounding above them as two sets of footsteps headed their way.

Rae glanced up towards the sound and automatically crouched her body over Luke's, protecting it as she put her free hand on his cheek. "Who's that?" she hissed between her teeth. "Do you think that could be—"

"It's Carter and Jennifer," Devon said quietly. "They must have heard the noise."

"How come we didn't?" Rae said suddenly, the guilty tears finally pouring over as she met his gaze. "There was a tremendous commotion in here! How come we didn't—"

"Rae," Devon flushed, "we were making quite the commotion ourselves."

Rae's heart tightened as she stared down at Luke, lying prone between them. If there was ever a betrayal in the world, this was it.

Just then, the door burst open and Carter and Jennifer came rushing inside. Their eyes grew wide as they took in the damage before falling on Rae, Luke, and Devon huddled in the center.

"What the hell happened?" Carter demanded as they rushed forward.

Jennifer quickly assessed Luke's condition then gave Rae a reassuring squeeze. "I think he's going to make it," she said softly. She shook her head with a disbelieving whistle. "It's a miracle, he's lost a hell of a lot of blood."

"I don't understand." Carter knelt down beside them. "What happened in here? And why is he here?" His eyes flashed up. "Your..."

"College counselor," Rae finished firmly. She glared up with a ferocity she didn't know she possessed and Carter seemed to back down. Out of embarrassment from his recent behavior or from the look Rae was giving him, she didn't know.

"Of course," he finished mildly. "Well then, help is just a few minutes out. They're going to bring him to the nearest hospital. I'm sure he'll be fine."

Rae nodded shakily and Devon squeezed her hand. "Here." He offered to take her blood-stained cardigan. "Do you want me to take over for a minute?"

"No." She pulled herself together. "I've got it. But thanks."

"I don't understand what he was doing here, in PC lodgings." Carter glanced around the living room. "And what the hell happened to this place?" He turned to Devon expectantly.

Devon shot Rae the quickest of glances as he scrambled to come up with something to say.

"I don't know," he admitted. "Rae and I were—out. We didn't hear a thing."

Whether Carter heard the slight hitch in his voice, it was impossible to say. Jennifer, on the other hand, definitely heard it. She flashed Rae a look but turned her eyes to the room instead.

"Whatever it was they were after, it's probably safe to assume they didn't get it," she said quietly. "Nothing's really stored here. Everything of value is back at the base."

Devon nodded. "That's what I thought too."

"So what about him?" Carter pointed at Luke. "He just got in the way?"

"Looks like it," Jennifer muttered.

"But why was he here in the first place?"

"Because he's a friend!" Devon snapped, ending the back and forth. Carter looked at him sharply, but let it go, averting his gaze with belated, debriefing guilt.

No one said a thing after that.

Jennifer and Carter stared around at the room, Devon stared at Rae, and Rae stared at Luke—stroking his face, silently begging him to wake up.

She just couldn't believe this was happening. Last night, she was attacked at a ball. Early this morning, she'd seen her mother's face for the first time in decades. This afternoon, she and Devon...she refused to let herself think about it while she was holding a cloth to Luke's head. Then this evening, Luke was nearly beaten to death in her makeshift living room, while she lay in the room beside. How could she have not heard or one of her tatùs not sense it?

It was too much! Everything was happening too fast, unraveling too quickly. How could she be expected to keep up?

Finally a few minutes later, the incoming sound of sirens roused them to their feet.

"All right, let's carry him down," Carter instructed. "Be careful to brace his neck."

He reached out to help, but Devon withdrew from his open hand so fast it was like he'd been burned. Their eyes met for a brief second before Carter flushed crimson and looked away.

"It's okay," Devon muttered, "I got him."

Ever so gently, he lifted Luke into the air and started carrying him to the door—careful not to disturb his position in the slightest. Rae walked along beside them, keeping her sweater pressed firmly to Luke's head to stem the bleeding. The steady drip that trailed behind them told her that no matter how sincere her efforts, she wasn't doing a good job.

"He just won't stop bleeding," she whispered in panic as they carried him down the stairs to the front lawn. "Devon, he came here to tell me something, and now I can't get him to stop bleeding."

"It's all right," Devon reassured her again as paramedics rushed towards them, "these guys know what they're doing. He's going to be okay."

Luke was lifted away from them and placed in the back of a Privy Council ambulance. It was unlike anything Rae had ever seen. Jet black, armor-plated—and inside—armed to the teeth.

"I don't understand," standing in the midst of a swarm of frantic people, she suddenly felt tiny, "is that for saving people or killing people?"

"Excuse me, miss." One of the paramedics pushed past her. "Does he have any family members or superior officers who'll be riding with us?"

Rae looked up hopefully and Carter gave her a small nod.

"Me!" she exclaimed, hopping into the back of the van. "I'm going with him."

As the doors closed she caught Devon staring at her from the other side of the glass. For a split second, she thought he might be angry with her eagerness. However, there was no time to think about it. The engine revved and the doors hummed with the vibration. A minute later, they were flying down the streets of London.

Although she'd traveled these roads enough to know them like the back of her hand, Rae had never seen them like this. The traffic congestion from yesterday's royal event had the entire city in some sort of lockdown. Roadblocks and overworked police officers directed people through detour after detour until Rae thought she'd pull out her hair from the stress.

"Can't we go any faster?" she demanded, holding Luke's hand tightly in her own.

"I'm sorry, miss," a paramedic said in reply. "Even with the sirens, we're merely being directed through the 'faster' detours. There are few things the government takes more seriously than the safety of the royal family."

Rae shook her head and pressed her free hand up against the window. "Don't I know it."

After about two hours in the van, they finally pulled up to the hospital loading dock. Luke was shuffled out on his stretcher as Rae hovered alongside him, doing her best not to get lost in the crowds. Despite her protests, Luke was quickly wheeled away to the ICU and she was relegated to the main lobby to wait for news of his condition. It was sheer torture.

Not knowing what was happening to him now. Not knowing what *had* happened just a few hours before. The only thing she did know was that no matter the details, she was at the center of this whole catastrophe. She was culpable in all this—whether she knew what was happening or not.

Time began to stretch on and distort. There was not a word about Luke, and Carter, Jennifer, and Devon had yet to arrive. Not that she expected them to. If they had to use the regular channels like everyone else, it could be days before they got here.

In a fit of nerves, she finally collapsed into a chair beside the water cooler, watching a group of rowdy kids crowded around the registration desk. Her head fell into her hands with a tired sigh.

How much longer could this possibly take?

"What are you in for, honey?"

Rae jumped as a kindly old woman patted her comfortingly on the arm.

"Oh...um..." Her mind came up blank and she bit her lip to stop the tears. "I'm not really sure," she whispered. "I'm not really sure what happened."

The woman nodded understandingly. "I'm here for my son, Jimmy. Gallstones. Third time in four months, if you can believe it." She lowered her voice soothingly. "Is it something like gallstones?"

Rae stared at her for a moment, before collecting herself. "No, it's nothing like gallstones."

The woman nodded and pulled some throat lozenges out of her purse. One of them got away from her and rolled onto the floor.

"Here," Rae offered, "let me get that for you." She bent down to pick it up and the base of her shirt pulled up, revealing her fairy tatù. When she handed the lozenge back to the woman, she was surprised to see that her entire demeanor had changed.

She looked at Rae the way someone looked at a stray dog that might be a little dangerous. "I don't approve of ink art," she sniffed and turned her eyes front.

Rae bit back a sarcastic response and sighed again. *The ol' tramp stamp judgement.* "You know what," she said too softly for the woman to hear, "I'm starting to agree with you."

One hour stretched into two. Rae switched to Devon's tatù to sharpen her senses, so when she heard a doctor across the noisy hall say Luke's name, she nearly knocked people down in her rush to get over.

"You have news on Luke?" she said breathlessly. "I'm the one who came in with him. Is he going to be okay? What's happening?"

A doctor took her gently by the arm and gestured to a small, side room. "Here, let's talk somewhere a bit quieter, away from prying ears."

Rae followed obediently as he led her inside and closed the door firmly behind him. She was about to start pelting him with more questions when a mark on his inner arm froze her in her tracks. It was a small, symmetric pile of bones. Almost like a pirate, but more deliberate. Clinical. In fact, the more she looked at it, the more it reminded her of something she'd seen before.

"You...you have a tatù," she said in amazement. She'd known that the Privy Council had people everywhere, she just hadn't imagined that this doctor could be one of them.

"That's why the PC brought your friend to this hospital, despite its distance from where you were staying."

"I have a friend who has a similar mark," Rae said, putting two and two together.

"Alecia." The doctor's eyes lit up as he smiled. "She works with us now too. She's one of our most promising students."

Whatever the circumstance, Rae found herself strangely comforted that there were people here with abilities like she had. People working to make Luke well. That is, she was comforted until she heard the doctor's next words.

"I'm sorry," Rae shook her head like a child, "a subdural hema—what?"

"It's a brain bleed," the doctor explained. "Your friend is bleeding inside his skull and it's putting pressure on his brain. We're going to need to do surgery to relieve the pressure."

The room seemed to tilt and Rae put her hand on the wall to steady herself. "Well is it... I mean, could it be life threatening? Is it a common procedure? What are his chances here?"

"It's brain surgery," the doctor said kindly. "Whenever the brain is involved, there's an enormous risk. The good news is, we think we caught it in time. We're prepping him for surgery now, just waiting for a call from the blood bank."

Whenever the brain is involved, there's an enormous risk.

Rae's head was spinning. "I'm sorry...the blood bank?"

The doctor put his hand on her shoulder. "Luke lost a great deal of blood and you caught us right after a significant national event with this ball the Royals were throwing. You heard about it?"

"I heard about it," Rae echoed faintly.

"Anyway, we're in short stock, and I'm hesitant to put him under until we have a full supply. Do you know if he has any family nearby? Is there someone we should inform?"

"I don't...I don't know..."

"Rae!"

She looked behind her to see Devon running ahead of Carter and Jennifer. She collapsed into his arms with a small gasp. "Thank goodness. I think I was about to fall over."

"So what's the prognosis?" Devon asked with concern. "Is he going to be okay?"

"He needs blood," Rae bit her lower lip, "he needs blood and they don't have any."

"I'll donate," he said instantly. He turned to the doctor. "I'm O-negative, universal donor. I can do it right now."

"That would be wonderful." The doctor gestured him down the hall. "Right this way."

"Devon..." Rae didn't know what to say, "...thank you."

He squeezed her hand and winked. "Anytime."

As he disappeared around the corner, Rae turned back to the doctor. "Do you think I could see him? Luke, I mean. Before you take him into surgery?"

"That's not exactly standard practice," the doctor hesitated. "You're not family."

"I'm the only person he's got."

She stared at him with wide, teary eyes before he finally conceded.

"Fine," he said, pointing her to a room behind a thick set of double doors. "But only for a minute. He needs to rest."

"Thank you so much! Only for a minute!" she promised.

She darted through the doors then abruptly slowed down as she saw Luke lying on the bed in front of her. He was pale as a sheet. Tied to a million ominous machines by a tangle of tubes and needles stuck deep in his skin. A shrill beeping coming from the nearest one assured her that his heart was still beating, but she wouldn't have believed it if she hadn't heard it for herself.

"Oh Luke," she murmured. She perched on a chair beside his bed and took him as gently as she could by the hand. "I'm so, so sorry about all of this. I don't know why you were in my place, but I know you are the victim here. You didn't deserve any of it!" The steady machine beeped back at her and she winced. "I promise, I'm going to figure out who did this to you. I'm going to figure it out, and I'm going to make them pay!" She glanced up at his face, half expecting him to speak, but all he did was lie there. Clinging to life in a hospital far from home. *It's all my fault!*

He had showed up today because of *her*. This had happened in *her* house—just down the freaking hall! She hadn't come out to stop it because she and Devon... What if he had heard them? What had happened?

Silent tears slipped down and landed on their enjoined hands.

"Great," she whispered. "Now I'm crying on you." She reached down to wipe them away when she noticed something crinkled up in Luke's fist. A paper of some kind. Something he'd obviously been trying to deliver. Something he'd attempted to hide when he was attacked.

As delicately as she could, she extracted it from his sleeping fingers. It was crinkled up and torn, but there was definitely writing on the back of it. Scribbled in a rushed hand. She was about to unfold it when heavy footfalls told her the doctors were on their way in. Instead, she stuffed it into the back pocket of her jeans and kissed Luke swiftly on the cheek.

"You're going to make it through this just fine," she promised quietly. "And I'm going to be right here when you wake up."

"I'm sorry, Miss Kerrigan, we need to take him away now."

"Okay," she got to her feet, "thanks again for letting me come inside."

She watched as they lifted him from one bed to the next and rolled him away towards the restricted doors at the end of the hall. A lump rose up in her throat, but she kept herself together and made herself watch until he had completely disappeared.

She would find out who did this, she swore it to herself like she'd sworn to him. An attack on one of her friends was an attack on her. She would not let it go unnoticed. She would not let Luke bleed for nothing. Whoever was responsible was out there, probably planning their next move.

The crumpled paper pressed hard against her skin and the tatù on her back seemed to almost burn in anticipation.

Whoever they were, whatever they wanted...she would be waiting for them.

Chapter 10

Leaving one man bleeding in the room behind her, Rae went off to find another bleeding in a room down the hall. She didn't know what, if anything, was on this mysterious note burning a hole in her pocket, but she did know one thing for sure. She couldn't face it alone.

Devon was sitting up in a stiff upholstered chair, watching as a bloody tube coming out of his arm filled up a small plastic bag hanging over his head. Two more bags were already filled and lying on a counter beside him.

"Hey." Rae tried to smile as she slipped inside and perched on the counter, careful not to disturb the bags. "How's it going in here? How're you feeling?"

"Oh," Devon smiled faintly in return, "good, everything's going good. How's Luke?"

"They just wheeled him into surgery." Rae frowned, examining Devon. His eyes were slightly unfocused and his head kept tilting sleepily to the left. "Are you sure you're okay?"

Devon blinked slowly and stared at her for a bit longer than what was normal before answering. "I'm fine. They just took quite a bit of blood is all." He played absentmindedly with the edge of his shirt and swung his legs against the base of the chair like a small child.

Rae couldn't help but smile. "Oh, boy." She hopped off the counter and ran her fingers comfortingly through his dark hair. "Looks like you're pretty out of it, huh?"

Devon closed his eyes and grinned as she continued stroking his forehead. "That feels nice."

"You know, you probably saved Luke's life by doing this." Her eyes tightened. "I...I don't really know how to thank you."

"Just keep doing what you're doing." Devon had the same sleepy smile on his face. "But don't talk so fast—it's hard to keep up."

Rae stifled a chuckle as the nurse came in.

"All right Mr. Wardell," she said, all business-like, "time to get you unhooked." She gently extracted the needle and took down the bag above his head before suddenly noticing the two more sitting on the counter. "What's this?" she demanded, gesturing to them. "Are those yours? Who on earth let you donate three whole pints?!"

Devon's head lolled to the side and he regarded the nurse with mischievous triumph. "I conned the other two nurses who came in before you—told them I was still waiting to donate."

Rae smacked his shoulder in disbelief. "Why the hell did you do that? That's dangerous!"

"Ow." He rubbed at the bruise pitifully. "They said Luke was in bad shape—that he needed a lot and they didn't have it in the blood bank. I just wanted to help..."

His voice trailed off and Rae and the nurse shared an exasperated, mildly panicked look.

"I'll just...go and get him a cookie and some juice," the nurse volunteered quickly. She apparently wasn't eager for the administration to discover her co-workers' mistakes. "You just sit tight, honey."

"Like I'm going to go anywhere," Devon muttered as she vanished through the door.

Despite the dramatic loss of blood, he kept his eyes open and tried to sharpen up and look alive as he stared around the room. His fingers pulled distractedly at the gauze the nurse had placed in the crook of his elbow and Rae was quick to stop him. He didn't even notice.

"That was a really dumb idea," she said gently, squeezing his hand. "What am I supposed to do with a boyfriend that displays constant selfless disregard for his own well-being?"

Devon smiled again, peering up at her as he rested his head against the chair. "You called me your boyfriend."

Rae's cheeks flushed, but she didn't break eye contact. "Well, after what happened this afternoon, I'd certainly hope you are."

"Is that right?" He squeezed her hand back and winked. "Well then, your boyfriend I will have to be." They held each other for a moment, before his face grew suddenly serious. "So when will you know anything about Luke? What did they say was wrong with him?"

Rae sighed. "It's a brain bleed. They're doing surgery to relieve the pressure. It's supposed to take a couple of hours."

Devon nodded calmly. "Okay, well we'll be here. You can be right here when he wakes up."

"You don't have to be so nice about it," Rae muttered, staring down at her hands. "I know you don't like him. You don't have to, I mean, you were draining yourself of blood just to—"

"Hey," he cut her off. "Your friends are my friends. Your problems are my problems. Since Luke is one of your *friends*," he put a slight emphasis on the last word, "I'll always do whatever I can to help. For you, Rae."

For you, Rae. That was exactly the problem.

A sudden wave of guilt crashed over her and she pulled away. "Please don't be rushing off to get yourself hurt on my account. There's been quite enough of that lately."

Devon frowned. "Honey, this wasn't your fault."

"And how's that?" Rae demanded. "*I* asked Luke to dig through the Xavier Knights files on my mom. *I* almost set fire to his apartment when I met up with him in London to get the box, and *I* asked him to check on the security feeds from the night she went missing."

"How did you almost set fire to his apartment—"

"It's not important, Devon. What's important is the one common denominator in all of these problems is me. I mean...Lanford, Kraigan. *I'm* the one repeatedly putting everyone around me in danger."

Devon frowned. "You can't think of it like that. *Lanford* and *Kraigan* put everyone in danger, not you. You didn't ask for any of this. The whole time I've known you, you've only ever wanted to do the right thing. Find out who you are."

"But at what cost?" Rae wiped a dot of blood off his smooth skin. "I never wanted anyone to get hurt." She gave him an appraising stare for a second, before reaching into her pocket and pulling out the folded piece of paper.

"What's that?" he asked.

"It was crumpled up in Luke's hand," she explained. "I think he was trying to bring it to me when he was attacked. I think this is what they were after. Well, this and my mom's files."

Devon tried to pull himself up straighter. "What does it say?"

"I don't know, I can't bring myself to look." Rae tucked her hair nervously behind her ears. "It doesn't feel right somehow. With Luke still in surgery."

"Rae, Luke's lying there because he risked everything trying to give this to you. You have to open it. You owe it to him!"

Rae hadn't thought of it that way. She'd just assumed that the search would continue once Luke was in the clear. But Devon was right. What was Luke's sacrifice for, if not this?

With trembling fingers, she unfolded the paper and looked down at the rapid script below. It was an address, preceded by a few scribbled words in Luke's hand:

There's somebody here I think you should meet:
559 Rue Étoiles
Marquise, FR

It couldn't be...could it?

Rae read the little note over and over, gripping the paper so tight the edge of it started to tear. After all this time, after all of the blood and tears it took to get to this point, had Luke just confirmed what her heart had been screaming at her for the last few days?

Was her mother really alive?

"Is that what I think it is?" Devon had been reading over her shoulder but fell back against the pillow in an exsanguinated haze. "Is your mom in France?"

Rae took a deep breath. Her tatù glowed warmly again and a slow smile crept up the side of her face. "There's only one way to find out."

"Really Devon, of all the days for you to go and drain *all* your blood."

Rae was shuffling along, toeing a clumsy and exhausted Devon along beside her. She had thrown his arm over her shoulder, but despite her strength tatù, they were still struggling.

"Oh I'm sorry," he slurred. "I'm sorry that this came at a bad time for you. Maybe the next time I decide to save your friend's life, I'll make sure it's scheduled for your convenience."

Scheduled for your *convenience*?

Rae shot him a tortured glance out of the corner of her eye, but said nothing. Typical luck, really. Now that she finally had a concrete address (hopefully her mother's) in France, she was literally limping towards it at a crawl. Furthermore, she had no idea how they were supposed to get out of the city with the gridlocked traffic blocking every street. Not to mention, Devon—while trying to get out of the chair and failing four times—had told her that Carter had driven him and Jennifer to the hospital in his own car, so if they wanted to get to France, they'd have to take a cab.

Could cabs legally cross the Chunnel? How much would that even cost?

Devon took that moment to trip on his own shoe, and they both almost went down before Rae pulled them back up to standing.

Nope, right now, their luck pretty much sucked all around.

"Karen?"

Rae and Devon kept shuffling down the hall.

"Karen!"

Oh shit, that's me!

Rae whirled around to see the future Queen of England waving at her from a restricted room on the other side of the hall. Flanking her on all sides were a dozen or so bodyguards, suited and unsmiling, little corkscrew cords coming out of radios stuck deep in their ears. Standing behind them all, like a watchful mountain, was the young lady's personal bodyguard, Alfie.

"Sarah?"

Rae limped into the room, tugging Devon along behind her. If the image struck the bodyguards as strange, they certainly didn't let on. In fact, they made no move as Rae and Devon approached Sarah's examination chair—they must not have looked like much of a threat.

Rae's eyes grew wide as she looked at the future queen. "Sarah, what are you doing here?"

Sarah turned to Alfie with what looked almost like muted triumph. "That's a damn good question. What am I doing here, Alfie?"

Alfie turned beet red but kept his eyes forward. "We're covering all our bases, miss."

Sarah rolled her eyes. "Alfie decided that even though *I'm just fine*, I had to come in and be seen by a doctor for residual drug effects after the attack at the ball."

That actually sounded quite logical to Rae, but she kept her mouth shut since Sarah was clearly not having it. Instead, she took a brief moment to draw a mental comparison between herself and this future queen. Physically, they were complete opposites. Both were slender and petite, but while Sarah was blond and blue-eyed, Rae's dark raven hair cascaded around her shoulders in unruly curls. Both had important, exclusive jobs— the Privy Council and the Royal Family—but while Sarah's duties would entail a lot of ribbon-cutting and policy discussion, Rae was constantly in the line of fire. Dodging psychotic teachers and family members—rescuing her boyfriend from the brink of death as she broke into a museum and tried to locate a missing brainwashing device.

Actually, she wondered if Sarah could officially pardon her for the whole museum thing...

But now was not the time.

"Well, I'm sure it will be over and done with before you know it," Rae said quickly, while trying not to be rude. "I wish you the best of luck. And, I believe we're supposed to see each other to go over your new security measures on Monday, correct?"

"Yes that's correct but..." Sarah's inquisitive eyes travelled briefly over the tired bruises under Rae's eyes and came to rest on Devon, half-sleeping on top of her. "Is everything...all right?"

"This?" Rae stepped on Devon's foot and his eyes snapped back open. "Oh yes, everything's fine. Just a little training exercise gone awry. You know how these things go."

She was rambling. She rambled when she was nervous.

She made a concerted effort to stop talking as Sarah briefly studied her face. Even in a hospital gown, Sarah still looked like royalty. She was sitting on the exam table with perfect posture, like it was already a throne. When she spoke, her voice demanded nothing but strict, immediate compliance. "Gentlemen, leave us."

As one, the bodyguards filed out of the room, taking up position outside, no doubt. Only Alfie stayed behind. Staring calmly ahead as if the rules didn't apply to him.

"Alfie..." Sarah coaxed. He looked at her, startled, and she gave him a sweet smile. "I need to speak to my friends for a moment."

"Absolutely not," he said without hesitation.

Sarah stifled a fond smile. "You know I outrank you, right?"

"No, miss. That was never explained to me."

She chuckled and pointed to the door. "Out. I'll be perfectly safe with these two. And we'll only be a moment, you have my word."

With a look of the utmost disapproval, Alfie slowly walked out the door—keeping his head held high. On the way out, he glanced down at Rae and Devon, still struggling to stand.

"Not sure they'd be much help in terms of protecting..." he murmured, and shut the door.

Once the three of them were alone, Sarah smiled graciously and gestured for Rae and Devon to sit. "Please, get off your feet. It looks like he needs it," she added quietly.

With a grateful nod, Rae lowered Devon into a chair before sinking into one herself. She hadn't realized how exhausted she was until she got off her feet for a moment.

"Now tell me," Sarah leaned forward with a look of genuine concern, "what's going on?"

"It has nothing to do with you," Rae quickly reassured her. "It's...personal." She was about to let it go with that, but the weight of the last two days suddenly caught up with her and felt the uncontrollable need to spill. "It's about my mother."

"Your mother?" Sarah repeated. "I thought...pardon me, Karen, but I thought your mother had passed away."

"So did I. So did everybody. And...it's Rae, actually."

"Rae." Sarah grinned. "Please continue."

"Last night I got word that while my father surely died in the fire, my mother might actually be alive and living in France. I got the address just now from a friend who almost died trying to pass me the information... Devon and I are on our way there right now. Well," she glanced down at him dozing on the counter beside her, "we're trying our best."

Sarah followed her gaze. "What's wrong with him," she whispered.

Rae shook her head with a smile. "It's a long story. But he'll be right as rain once we get his blood sugar back up. And his blood level...for that matter."

Sarah nodded as if this was the most normal thing in the world. But she suddenly looked down at her hospital gown as if it was a cage, keeping her there.

"This is so frustrating," she murmured. "I want to help you— the two of you have done so much for Philip and me. But with the press outside watching my every move, I don't know how I can be of much use..."

Rae shook her head quickly. "Don't worry about it—I would never ask that of you. You just focus on keeping yourself safe. We'll see you on Monday."

But Sarah was in her own world, lost in thought. "There's nothing I can do..." she repeated, "but maybe there's something I can give you to help." Her face suddenly brightened as she called, "Alfie! Stop eavesdropping and get in here!"

The door burst open and Alfie rushed in on a wave of adrenaline, gun drawn and pointed. "What is it?! What's the matter?!"

"I wish you'd stop doing that," Sarah said seriously.

"Sorry mum, old habits."

He headed over to her side and leaned down as she whispered something in his ear. He frowned disapprovingly, but she raised her eyebrows to insist, and without a word, he headed out a back entrance to the parking lot. Half a minute later, he returned and slipped something into Sarah's hands, something Sarah immediately offered to Rae.

"Flags?" Rae held out the tiny patriotic flags and waved them doubtfully. "Look, I know that since you're so close to a royal wedding and a coronation you're probably a bit overwhelmed with nationalistic fervor, but I don't see how this—"

"They're diplomatic flags," Sarah giggled as she explained. "From our town car. Wherever you're going, they'll let you get waved on through. Without them, I don't see how you'd even make it out of the city tonight."

Rae suddenly looked down at the flags as if they were a life raft, a precious token taking her to where she needed to be. She touched the fabric gently and then looked up at Sarah, grateful beyond words.

"Thank you, Sarah. *Really*. You don't know how much this means to me."

"Go," Sarah said, her eyes twinkling with merriment. "On Monday, you're going to have to tell me all about it."

Rae nodded and heaved Devon to his feet before shuffling to the door.

They had just gotten out to the hall when Sarah suddenly called out to them. "Rae..." she paused, "somehow I think your life is going to be much more interesting than mine."

"I highly doubt that, your future highness." Rae grinned. "But we'll see."

"Yes," Sarah grinned back, "we certainly will."

Armed with her diplomatic immunity, Rae took off at a quicker pace, calling on Jennifer's tatù to help her shoulder Devon's weight. They passed by countless doctors and nurses, but fortunately, no one seemed to ask where these two teenagers, one with what looked like serious coordination problems, were going. They had almost made it to the back exit when a flash of crimson hair caught Rae's eye.

"Molly?" she called incredulously.

Molly whirled around and barreled towards them. "Rae! I came as soon as I heard! Oh my goodness! I can't believe it!

How's Luke? Is he okay? Wait! What happened to Devon? Is he okay? I just saw Carter and Jennifer but I didn't talk to them yet, I wanted to find you guys." She suddenly stretched up on her tiptoes to examine Devon's face. "Rae Kerrigan. That is your lip gloss he's wearing. I'd know it anywhere. I bought you the shade. What happened last night? Looks like you two worked out your issues after all, huh? Wait!" Her eyes grew wide. "Just how well did you work them out...if you know what I mean?!"

Rae had to literally grab her by the shoulders to get her to stop talking. "Molls, take a breath! Devon's fine, Luke's in surgery. Now back up for a minute, did you say you just saw Carter and Jennifer?"

"Yeah, they were just up near the ICU looking for you guys. Why? Rae, what's going on?"

Rae grabbed Molly's hands and pulled her close. "Luke got me an address. I think it's for my mom. Molly, you have to help me."

Molly's eyes shone with excitement. "Of course I will! Tell me what you need me to do!"

Rae cast an anxious glance up and down the hall. Any minute, Carter and Jennifer could spot them. While Rae knew Carter had some lingering guilt over the way he'd acted that morning, she didn't think either of them would allow her and Devon leave to go trotting off to France while they were on probation and the city was in virtual lockdown.

"I need you to cover for us with Carter. Tell him—I don't know—tell him Devon donated too much blood to save Luke and I'm taking him back to Heath Hall because he's ill."

It was half true. Devon had clearly lost too much blood and they were going away.

"Sure, no problem," Molly promised, rising to the challenge. "In the meantime, just be safe, okay Rae?" She suddenly jumped on her in an excited embrace. "And congratulations! I mean, by this time tomorrow, you could be talking to your mother!"

Rae shook her head in amazement, suddenly a bit dizzy herself. "I know, I can't believe it!"

There was a sudden commotion down the hall and she and Molly looked up to see a rush of doctors pour inside as an incoming patient was transferred to the ICU.

"Okay, I gotta go!" Rae secured her grip and Devon's arm and started pulling him towards the door. "Molly, there's one more thing." She bit her lip and tried to keep it together. "Will you keep an eye on Luke for me?"

Molly's face softened and she nodded her head. "Of course I will. You can count on me."

"Thanks!" Rae said gratefully as she tugged Devon through the double doors and out into the parking lot. Despite her unparalleled heap of bad luck, she had truly lucked out with a friend like Molly. It was always in times of stress when you realized how great it was to know that someone out there had your back. Unconditionally.

Devon was waking up, slowly but surely, and he helped Rae along as they weaved through parked cars, trying desperately to spot a taxi. Rae briefly considered how strange it was going to look, a city cab with diplomatic flags sticking off the sides, but she would worry about that later. All she was focused on now was getting her and Devon off the street before anyone could stop them.

"Miss Skye?"

A booming voice stopped her dead in her tracks and she automatically switched to a different tatù, using her super-hearing to eavesdrop through the hospital wall.

It was Carter. He had apparently found Molly still hovering near the nurse's station. Rae bit her lip anxiously as her eyes darted around for a cab. They had to get out of here—*now*!

"What're you doing at the hospital?" Carter asked curiously. "I thought you'd gone back to Guilder."

"I was going to," Molly stumbled, "I mean, I did. Then I heard about Luke and I wanted to make sure he's okay."

Devon pressed his ear against the wall as well, listening with his own tatù.

"Have you seen Mr. Wardell and Miss Kerrigan?" Carter asked impatiently. "I've been trolling the halls but I can't find them."

"Yeah I did." Molly tried to sound convincing. "Actually, donating blood made Devon a little sick so the two of them just headed back to base so he could sleep it off."

Rae could almost hear Carter frown.

"How are they getting back to Heath Hall? I drove here."

It had to be said, for all her talents, Molly truly sucked at improvising. Rae held her breath as she floundered. "Well, I think they were just going to grab a taxi out in front."

There was a second's pause and Rae smacked her forehead, recognizing Molly's mistake at the same time that Carter did.

"Taxis come around the back..."

"Shit!" Rae silently cursed. "Come on, Devon! We've got to go!"

Together, they half-jogged, half-limped to the other side of the parking lot and crouched behind a parked SUV. A row of taxis was making its way slowly down the street in front of them and Rae tentatively stuck out her arm. If she could just catch one's attention and get it to curve around, maybe she and Devon could slip inside without—

A tall shadow fell over them and Rae looked up in horror to see Carter standing there, his long arms crossed over his chest.

"Where on earth do you two think you're going?"

Chapter 11

Carter and Rae were locked in a standoff, staring each other down in the late afternoon sun, neither of them surrendering so much as an inch. As the evening breeze stirred her curls around her, Rae brought herself up to her full height. Carter could interrogate her all he wanted. She was never going to say a damn thing.

"It's going to be okay, Rae," Devon whispered loudly, "just don't tell him about France."

Rae shut her eyes in a painful grimace as Carter stared at Devon in complete disbelief.

"France? Did he just...?" he asked. "Miss Kerrigan, what the hell is going on?"

"I'm dating an exsanguinated idiot," Rae muttered under her breath.

Carter leaned forward with a frown. "What's that?"

"Nothing," Rae said swiftly. She gestured to Devon's wilted form. "He's not himself. He conned the nurses into letting him donate way too much blood. We're just heading back to Heath Hall now to let him sleep it off."

"Nice cover." Devon winked.

Oh, for Pete's sake. How was she supposed to go anywhere like this?! The diplomatic flags were still clutched in her fist, and for a minute, she considered stashing Devon somewhere safe and just waving them around as she started walking.

Carter raised his eyebrows, unimpressed with their new tactic of lie, then self-expose. A taxi slowed down tentatively on the street beside them, but he waved it away with a flick of his wrist. Rae stared after it, watching her chance of seeing her mom drive off into the sunset. She followed it all the way until it disappeared before Carter reclaimed her attention.

"Rae," he spoke softly and used her first name, "I think you should tell me what's going on."

Her shoulders slumped as she sighed. They had been caught. There was no way around it. It was time to face the music.

Before anyone could say a thing, Devon suddenly gripped the side of Rae's neck as his legs buckled and threatened to give way beneath him. She quickly lowered him down to sit on the grass by the curb. Carter rushed forward and took his other arm to help. It was a testament to how out of it Devon really was that he didn't struggle or pull away when Carter reached out to touch him. Instead, he just gripped the fabric on his boss' sweater with a thoughtful look on his face.

"That's really soft," he murmured quietly.

All at once, Rae's heart seized up in her chest. Devon's mind was completely defenseless, an open book. Distorted and hazy. Who knows what Carter would be able to see without Devon trying to keep him at bay? What if he saw...?!

She glanced at Carter in a moment of blind panic only to see Carter look up at her at the same time. Her lips parted and she was about to say something—a denial, a reprimand—she didn't know, but before she could, Carter help up a peaceable hand.

"I didn't look, I didn't see a thing," he said softly. The tops of his cheeks flushed faintly in shame as he knelt down and helped Devon sit up straight. "I know you have no reason to believe that, but it's the truth."

But for whatever reason, Rae did believe him. In many ways, his face was as open as Devon's, laid bare by the mention of her mother, honestly trying to figure out what was going on.

"Luke isn't my college counselor," she admitted.

Carter rolled his eyes. "You don't say." But he kept his peace and listened quietly.

"He works for..." She hastily edited herself. "He's a bit of a computer genius and has access to a lot of information. He's the one that found me the box my mother left for me. It had some files and a video tape which we watched together."

Carter was leaning back on his heels, holding his breath as he absorbed every word. He was sure to have spotted some holes in her stories—some critical information she was omitting—but he let it go. Letting Rae tell the story as he silently listened.

"Anyway, the video was time stamped and Luke said he was going to check the footage from security tapes around the area to see if he could find any trace of my mom or any clue as to what happened. When he came to Heath Hall this afternoon, he had this in his hand."

In a rare moment of trust, Rae extended the note. Carter read it in silence, tracing the writing with his fingers as Rae had done. There was a strange look on his face Rae had never seen before. The look of a man beyond hope who was struggling to hope again. When he finally glanced back up at Rae, that hope had been replaced with steely determination.

"Who attacked him?"

Rae ran her hands through her hair in frustration. "That's what I don't know. Only a few people even knew about the box—and since the video self-destructed after we watched—the only thing I was able to take with me were some old mission files of my mom's. The files were missing when we discovered Luke passed out on the floor."

She decided not to mention the contents of the tape or the secret code embedded in the files. There were some things that for now, at least, she wanted to keep for herself. And lucky for her, Carter wasn't pressing.

He was quiet for a moment, thinking, before his face suddenly cleared back into the Carter Rae had grown to know and even trust over the years. The man in control. The man who could do just about anything.

"This is what we're going to do—" he began.

"What *we're* going to do?" Rae raised her eyebrows.

She hadn't realized this was a joint mission. But as long as Carter wasn't actively shutting her down, she didn't know if she could complain. After all, for the next few hours Devon was going to be pretty much out of the picture. It might help to have another cognizant adult on her side.

"I'm coming with you." There was not a shadow of doubt or shame on Carter's face as he stared Rae straight in the eye. "I loved your mother, Miss Kerrigan, once upon a time. I loved her with all my heart. I would move heaven and earth to find her."

Rae froze for a moment in surprise, before slowly nodding her head. She believed him. And because of those feelings, on this particular mission, there was no one she'd rather have on her side.

"So what's the plan?" she asked quickly, awaiting his instructions.

He gave her a rare smile. "Jennifer and Molly will stay here at the hospital to keep tabs on your friend. Protect him from any future attacks, and keep us updated on his status."

Rae was surprised his plan in any way included Luke. Now that she had the note and the files were gone, she didn't understand why Carter would find him at all relevant.

Her surprise must have shown on her face, because Carter paused thoughtfully before continuing. "I know he's important to you. I'm not going to leave him here defenseless." He briefly met her eyes, and in a moment of enlightenment, something clicked into place.

Carter cared about Rae too—because of her mother. Carter felt protective of her.

"Thank you," she murmured. "I appreciate that."

He nodded briskly and turned his attention to the bustling city. The problem of the inescapable traffic must have just occurred to him, because he suddenly frowned and rubbed his chin. "Now, we just need to find a way to get out of this city..."

"Actually," Rae triumphantly held out the diplomatic flags, "I may have an idea about that."

Carter's face lightened in relief before he suddenly froze. "Tell me you didn't steal these from the royal family."

"I didn't steal them," Rae bristled defensively, "I just borrowed them from Sarah."

Carter raised his eyebrows. "Sarah? You two are on a first name basis now?"

Rae felt the blood rising in her cheeks. "Well...if you can count 'Sarah to Karen' a first name basis." Probably best not to mention that other little secret. She was pushing the boundaries as is.

Carter simply shook his head. "Pick your battles, right?" he murmured to himself. "I'm going to pull my car around back. Wait right here with Devon. Tell no one where we are going. I'll be back in a minute."

As Carter disappeared around the corner, Devon leaned back against Rae's legs and gazed up at her with a sleepy smile. "Did I help?" he asked hopefully.

She smiled and stroked back his hair. "Actually babe, you helped a lot."

Exactly one minute later, Carter whirled around the corner in a jet black town car. The kind of car that just might believably have diplomatic immunity. He grabbed the flags out of Rae's hand and adhered them quickly to his hood before returning to help her with Devon.

"Open the door," he instructed as he placed his hands on Devon's back and helped him get to his feet. Rae looked on with concern as she pulled open the door to the back seat.

"I don't understand," she said anxiously, "he seems to be getting worse, not better."

"That's just because he's been on the move with nothing to replenish his system," Carter assured her. "Here," he tossed her a vitamin water from the front seat, "give him this, it'll help."

Rae helped tip the bottle into Devon's mouth until he was strong enough to hold it on his own. Then she climbed into the front seat as Carter pulled out of the parking lot.

"So, Miss Kerrigan," he dodged through pedestrians and cars alike, "to the airport or—"

"The Chunnel?" she interjected hopefully.

He flashed her a peculiar look before clearing his face and fixing his eyes on the road.

"The Chunnel it is."

Only about an hour later, Rae and Carter were parked in the Eurotunnel Shuttle, sitting in silence as Devon slept peacefully in the back seat. Carter had stretched the power of the diplomatic flags as far as both common decency and roadside assistance would allow, and they had made it here in record time. But now that the engine was off and they simply had to wait, the car was quickly filling up with a million unanswered questions.

Rae tried to break the awkward silence. "I came here once before, you know. To the Chunnel, I mean," she clarified as Carter shot her another strange look. "I can barely remember it, I was really small, but I remember being so excited and then so disappointed all at the same time. I'd thought that we'd be in some kind of underwater tube and I'd get to see dolphins and fish and stuff. I didn't realize it was a sealed compartment. My poor mom," she chuckled, "I must have been a nightmare when I found out."

"You went with your mother?" Carter asked with that same odd look on his face.

Rae frowned at him curiously but then shrugged. "I guess. Who else would have taken me?"

There was a weighty pause as Carter seemed to be struggling with something. He clenched his jaw and stared fixedly at the steering wheel, trapped in resigned silence, before he suddenly shook his head with a little sigh.

"*I* took you."

Rae's mouth fell open. "You what?!" Carter looked at her with something close to pity, but she shook her head in complete dismissal. "No you didn't. Why on earth would *you* take me to the Chunnel? I went with my mom."

Carter's voice was quiet. "You went with me. It was your fifth birthday and your mother and father were fighting. He had come home and done or said something horrible to set her off." He shook his head as he tried to remember the specifics. "I was in town on business and Beth called me up in tears. Asked me to come take you for the day so you wouldn't get caught in the middle of it. Said it was your birthday and she didn't want your only memory to be of your crazy father."

Rae listened in silent disbelief. When she'd first arrived at Guilder and had met Carter, she'd assumed she was meeting him for the first time. Why would she think otherwise? He'd certainly acted like it was the first time he was meeting her. But now what was she supposed to do with *this*?

"I loaded you up in my car and asked you where you wanted to go." His eyes grew almost warm as he remembered. "You didn't even pause—you said you wanted to go to the Chunnel. I headed straight there." His sudden chuckle made Rae jump. "And yes—you were very upset when you couldn't see the dolphins. But when we got to the other side, I bought you some ice cream at a rest break and you seemed to calm down. When your mother called to check in on us a few hours later, she couldn't believe I'd taken you to France. 'Babysitting my kid for a few hours doesn't mean skipping the country, James'," he quoted.

A lingering smile faded slowly off his face as he turned to Rae—still sitting dumbstruck in the seat beside him.

"So yes," he said in conclusion. "I took you."

There were so many things Rae wanted to say. So many questions she wanted answered. Why didn't Carter tell her these kinds of things when she first got to Guilder? Why did it seem to be the policy of everyone she'd ever met to keep seemingly innocuous secrets from her—secrets about her own past?

In that moment, Rae suddenly realized that it couldn't have mattered less. What was done was done. They were all here now. There was no going back.

Instead of ranting or interrogating, she simply glanced at Devon still dozing in the back seat before turning her eyes front.

"If I was to tell you that when we get there, I'd actually like some ice cream..."

"We're not pulling over."

"Understood."

The French city of Marquise was only about twenty minutes from the Chunnel, and despite Carter's previous statement, they did in fact pull over. Devon had woken up and was staring around, quite surprised he was in another country, and Rae and Carter realized none of them had eaten a thing since breakfast. Carter pulled into a pub and the three of them piled out and headed inside.

The first thing Rae did was head to the bathroom. There was a distinct possibility she was about to meet her long-lost mother and she realized she had no idea what she was even wearing.

Thank goodness she did.

Streaks of dried blood laced up her arms, making her look like some sort of serial killer, and there was a dark red stain from Luke's head wound on the side of her shirt.

"Great!" she muttered as she began scrubbing it furiously. "She's going to take one look at me and think I take after my dad."

Once she'd removed the bulk of the blood and rolled up her sleeves, she scooped up her hair into a stylish ponytail and gave herself a once over. It was lucky that she'd dressed for a debriefing today. She was still in the same sky blue shirt and fashionable slacks as before. And while she and Devon may have done their best to undermine it, her makeup was holding up remarkably well. Altogether, she'd have to say that she looked refined, grown up. Exactly the way she'd want her mother to see her.

If she was in fact going to see her today.

A flurry of butterflies filled her stomach, and she floated back to their table at the far end of the bar. Carter was at the counter ordering for the lot of them, so Rae slid into the booth next to Devon as they waited for him to return.

"Why didn't you tell me there was blood on me?" she hissed through her teeth.

He looked up at her in surprise. "I didn't notice," he said honestly. "I mean, lately you usually have at least a little. I guess it doesn't jump out at me anymore."

"What does that say about me?" Rae shook her head in dismay. "I only look like myself when I'm dripping in somebody else's blood? What a perfect way to present myself. I'm no better than freaking Kraigan." She crossed her arms over her chest and pouted.

Devon raised his eyebrows in alarm. "Slow down there, turbo. What on earth are you rambling about?"

Rae blew a loose curl off her face in a huff before casting a sideways glance at Devon. "I want to look... I don't know. I want to look like the daughter she left behind. Not some trained up, callous, killing machine for the Privy Council. Not like my dad."

Devon took her hands kindly and tilted her chin up to look at him. "First of all, and I've been trying to tell you for years now Rae, your dad *did not* work for the Privy Council. Most definitely not. Get it straight."

She couldn't help but giggle a little at his teasing.

"Second," he tucked the runaway curl behind her ear and stroked the side of her face. "You are the most beautiful, extraordinary, loving person I've ever met. If we do end up meeting your mom today, there's no way she's going to miss that. You just need to relax, sweetie."

Rae sighed and leaned into his arms when he offered. "I'm just nervous."

He kissed the top of her head. "I know. But it's going to be all right, I promise."

Just then, Carter came back carrying three trays of burgers. Rae and Devon slid automatically to opposite sides of the bench and Carter rolled his eyes. "Yep. Because that's still a *secret*, right?"

"I think it's a little soon for you to be making accusations." Devon glared at him.

Carter flushed, but pointed an authoritative finger at Devon's plate. "*You*—get your blood sugar up. I'm done carting you across international borders. And *you*," he pointed at Rae, "we need to figure out how you want to do this."

Rae nibbled on the end of a chip. "What do you mean?"

Carter paused and when he spoke, it looked like he was treading carefully. "Your friend got knocked out before he could tell us anything about the address on that note. It could be your mother, it could be someone that has information about your mother. It could..." his face grew suddenly grave, "Rae, it could be that you're walking straight into a trap."

"It's not a trap," Rae said firmly. "I trust Luke. If you're going to do this with us, you're going to have to trust me."

Carter studied her for a long moment before he nodded. "Fine. Then while you go to the door, I'll keep an eye on the front while Devon circles around back to monitor the perimeter. And use a strong tatù, Rae. We don't want to take any chances."

Much to the men's surprise, Rae broke out into a huge smile. Did she detect some stalling here? It looked like someone was just as nervous to see her mother again as she was.

"This isn't a covert mission," she reminded him gently, "this is a reunion. I'm not going to have the two of you going all black ops on my mom. You can both come to the front door, just like normal people."

Devon reached over and wiped something off the side of Rae's neck. "*Normal* people don't *normally* have someone else's blood on them," he teased.

Rae's hand clapped to the spot in terror. "I'm sure it's just ketchup."

Devon grinned. "I'm sure."

They finished eating quickly, and before Rae knew it, they were back in the car. No one said much of anything as they headed away from the town and out into the open countryside.

The roads got smaller and smaller as the houses grew farther and farther apart. Towering beech and oak trees shaded the side of the road, filtering the golden sunlight in a surreal, almost dream-like way. Rae pressed her face against the window. Could this little wonderland really have been where her mother was living all these years?

"Shouldn't you call your Uncle Argyle?" Devon asked suddenly.

Rae looked up in surprise. She actually hadn't even thought about it. After a moment's consideration, she shook her head. "I don't want to get his hopes up. I mean, I keep thinking we're going to see my mom, but Carter's right. We don't really know what's waiting for us."

In fact, the closer they got to their destination, the more convinced Rae became that their spectacular journey was only going to lead to another clue. It was too much to believe that her mother could really be just minutes away, tucked away in this magical looking scenery.

The nerves and butterflies had started to once again overtake her, when Carter suddenly pulled off the road and into the drive of a small cottage house. Nobody said anything and Rae stared out the window in amazement.

It looked like something out of one of the fairytales her mother used to read to her as a child. Flowering vines and ivy crept up the grey stone walls towards the thatched roof, and a million different wildflowers created an iridescent carpet to an old wooden door. The windows were thick-paned and clouded, but Rae could just make out a hint of a light shining somewhere inside.

"Rae."

Rae turned to see Devon and Carter looking at her expectantly—each of them with a soft, almost tender smile in their eyes. When she didn't speak, Devon squeezed her hand gently.

"Are you ready?"

Rae took another long look out the window, before she pulled in a deep breath and gathered herself together. She had been ready for this for a long, long time.

Without a word, she pulled open the door and headed up the cobblestone walkway. The men trailed at a respectful distance behind her.

What was she going to say?!

The question struck her with instant panic. In all of her wishing and planning, she hadn't considered what she would actually do if the dream ever came true. What would she say to this woman she'd been torn away from as a child? What words could possibly make up the distance between them?

But as she raised her hand to knock, the door pulled open from the other side and Rae said the only word that came to mind. As simple as it was unbelievable.

"*Mom.*"

Chapter 12

Time stopped as Rae's mouth fell open and her eyes filled with tears. It wasn't just the video-tape reminder or her absentminded recollections over the last ten years, her mother looked exactly like Rae remembered her.

Petite, like Rae, but strong and fit—able to take care of herself. A wild mane of dark curls, identical to the ones Rae struggled to control every morning. The same eyes, the same mouth. A warm, heart-shaped face that seemed always a second away from bursting into a smile. In a lot of ways, staring at her mom was like staring in the mirror at Rae's own reflection. Just a few years older.

Only now, the reflection was complete.

Then Bethany Kerrigan said the only words that could tear it all away.

"I'm sorry...who are you?"

Oh no... Please...no, no, no...

Rae bent over as if she'd been punched in the gut. The cute little house spun around her and she literally doubled-over and put her hands on her knees. As she melted back down the steps, the men surged forward. Devon gathered her immediately into his arms, while Carter simply stood in front of them—staring at Beth like he'd seen a ghost.

"I can't believe it," he muttered. His skin had gone shock white and his eyes dilated to their fullest extent. "I can't believe it. You're alive. All this time."

Beth looked at him like he might be crazy. She stepped back, ready to slam the door closed. "Of course I'm alive. Is this some kind of joke?" She leaned past him and fixed her eyes on Rae with concern. "Is she all right?"

Rae had managed to stand up, huddled in Devon's arms. When she saw her mother looking at her, she got caught in a full-body tremble and silently shook her head.

No. She was most definitely not all right. In fact, she thought she might be sick.

Devon took the cue and thought on his feet. "Actually no, Mrs....?"

"It's just miss, actually." Bethany straightened but kept her eyes trained on Rae. A slight crease formed in the center of her forehead, as if she thought she might have seen this troubled girl somewhere before. "Miss Landais. Why don't you come inside...?" She gestured to Rae with a concerned frown. "We'll get her some water. She doesn't look well."

Devon smiled graciously. "Thank you, that's very kind."

He had completely taken over talking for the bunch, as it seemed Carter was incapable of saying anything coherent and Rae had literally crumbled the second her own mother didn't recognize her face.

Keeping a supportive arm around Rae's waist, Devon followed Bethany into a modest country kitchen as Carter trailed behind. Rae glanced around as she was lowered down into a chair beside the table. It looked exactly how you'd think it would by looking at the outside. Decorated in light yellows and creams, it caught the last light of the vanishing sun and sparkled it back on the walls through a series of sun-catchers and prisms. Old bronzed pots hung in orderly fashion from a series of nails in the stucco walls while dried flowers and herbs dangled in a corner from the ceiling. She'd hoped to find something about her inside the house. Like a picture or some hidden agenda that she knew who Rae was. Nothing.

"I grow them myself." Bethany caught Rae looking and tried to coax a smile. "Rosemary, lavender, thyme. Do you cook?" she asked politely, mistaking Rae's interest with aptitude.

"No," Rae's voice came out scratchy and she quickly cleared her throat. "No, I don't cook."

Neither did her mother, as well as Rae could remember. On holidays and festive occasions, they had gone out. You couldn't catch them on a day when their fridge wasn't stuffed with Indian or Chinese leftovers.

"When did that start?" Rae couldn't help but ask.

"Me?" Bethany asked. "I've always done it, ever since I was a little girl." She spoke with complete confidence, but even as she did, the slightest of shadows passed over her face, as if sensing a vague disconnect.

Rae latched onto this shadow with sudden fervor, clinging to it with everything she had.

She had been caught off guard at the door—who wouldn't? You show up and your own mother doesn't recognize your face? It was enough to knock the wind out of anyone's sails. But what happened to Beth had been done *to* her. *Why doesn't she remember me?*

A woman didn't just show up after a decade of being thought deceased in a storybook cottage in France thinking herself an aspiring chef named Landais. She didn't just inexplicably not remember the face of her own daughter. There was more to the story. There was someone behind the curtain, pulling at the strings.

"Actually," Rae said with a smile, "instead of water, do you think I could have a cup of tea?"

Every night when she was growing up, her mother would make her a nightly cup of chamomile—Beth swore by it. Rae would sit on her lap and slowly sip it down as Beth combed out her messy curls before tucking her into bed. Even after all these years, it was one of the few things that could settle her stomach and calm her nerves.

"Sure." Beth looked surprised, but pleased. "I know I have a box here somewhere."

As she got up and began rummaging through the cupboards, Devon squeezed Rae's hand gently in his own. "Are you all right?" he asked too quietly for anyone else to hear. Not that they were listening. Beth was busy in the spices and Carter only had eyes for her. "Rae, I don't know what to do," he said with a touch of anxiety. "I don't know how to help you here."

"It's okay," Rae whispered back, keeping her eye fixed on her mom. "I'm working on it."

Beth returned a moment later with a steaming mug. Rae glanced at the label on the bag and couldn't resist a small smile. Chamomile. So her mother was still in there somewhere. They just had to find her.

"Thank you," she smiled and took a steaming sip. At once, a flood of memories went coursing through her and she dropped her eyes quickly to the tea so no one could see them fill with tears. When she looked up a moment later, she was fine.

Once it was clear that Rae was going to be all right, Beth perched on the edge of the table and regarded them all in a critical stare. "Well then, what can I help you people with today?"

There was a moment of silence as Devon and Carter shared a panicked look.

Rae, however, remained perfectly calm. "Actually, I was just feeling a little dizzy on my way back to school. Guilder. Have you ever heard of it?"

That same shadow passed across Beth's face but she shook her head. "No, I haven't."

Rae's heart sank a little but she kept going. "It's near London. We were just driving back there when I felt like I might faint so my..." she glanced at Carter apologetically out of the corner of her eye as she tried desperately to simplify things, "my dad pulled over."

Carter shot her a look of supreme agitation while Devon bit his lip and quickly dropped his eyes to the floor.

Beth missed the entire exchange. She stared at Rae like she was trying desperately to place her. The two of them locked eyes and Beth diverted her gaze with an embarrassed smile. "I'm sorry, I don't mean to stare," she murmured. "I just can't shake the feeling that I've seen you somewhere before." She brightened with a casual shrug. "It must be because we kind of look alike, right?"

"Must be," Rae mused, soaking in the precious details of her mother's face.

"You know," Beth continued, "my mother had frequent fainting spells. It started when she was pregnant with me and carried on through her entire life."

"Really?" Rae tried not to smile. She certainly *did* know that, hence her strategic story.

So the damage to Beth's memory only went back so far. She still remembered her mother and her life before meeting Simon and having Rae.

"Yeah, it's pretty draining," Rae continued her fabrication with the self-righteous suffering of a martyr. "I'm sorry to just barge in on you like this. I guess we should be getting on our way."

Beth frowned as she glanced out the window. Night had fallen and the world around them was growing darker by the minute. There were next to no road signs out this far in the country and she was obviously worried about Rae's weakened state.

Rae watched the dilemma present itself on her mother's face with bated breath. She almost wished she still had some blood on her to complete the 'defenseless girl' image.

"Where are you staying for the night?"

Carter glanced at Rae and took over, catching on to her scheme. "We have reservations at a place about two hours from here." He squinted out into the darkness with a speculative look. "I'll just need to find some sort of rest stop first so we can get a map..."

Rae watched as Beth silently struggled with the predicament. The inherent danger of allowing three strangers to sleep in her house, versus the well-being of a sickly young girl. In the end, her eyes fell on Rae and she seemed to make up her mind.

"That's nonsense," she waved her hand dismissively, "you three should stay here for the night. Save yourself the trouble of a hotel."

"We couldn't impose," Carter said at the same time Rae spoke.

"Are you sure?" Rae feigned a look of hesitation. "We wouldn't want to impose."

"Not at all." Bethany gave her a kind smile. "If you're anything like my mother, then you need to rest young lady. There's a room upstairs where you can sleep."

"That's so generous of you, thank you so much!" Rae exclaimed. At least now, while she came up with a plan to return her mom's memory, they'd be sleeping under the same roof. "I'm sure my dad will be fine on the couch, and my boyfriend can just come up with me."

"He most certainly will not!" Both Carter and Bethany said at the same time.

They glanced at each other in surprise before fixing their attention on opposite sides of the room. Rae smothered another smile and buried her face in her tea. It was worth a shot.

"Your boyfriend can sleep on the couch in the living room," Beth said sternly, giving Devon a once-over that made him straighten in a hurry. "And you," she flashed Carter a suspicious glance, "the one with the crazy eye twitch. *You* can sleep in the car."

Casting a triumphant glance at the men lingering behind her, Rae followed her mom up the stairs and down the hall to a small but cozy guestroom. A tall wooden dresser stretched up against one wall while gauzy, laced curtains hung over the windows that occupied the other. A neatly made bed sat in between them.

Rae fingered the thick, handmade quilt that covered the mattress. "Did you make this?"

Bethany shook her head. "It was here when I moved into this place a few years ago."

"Oh, yeah?" Rae's head cocked up in interest. "Where did you move from?"

Her mother's lips opened and closed like she was going to say something as the same dark shadow passed over her face. However, nothing came out. Strangely enough, she seemed even more perturbed by this than Rae was. Eventually, she simply shook her head with a quick smile and headed to the dresser.

"I'll get you some pajamas," she said softly, pulling out a pair of striped sweatpants and a periwinkle camisole. "Let's not bother the boys to go to the car for clothes now. If you like, I can wash what you're wearing so it'll be clean for you tomorrow."

"That would be wonderful, thanks," Rae answered, taking the pajamas and holding them up appraisingly against her body.

"What do you know?" Beth smiled. "A perfect fit."

Rae shook her head with a small smile herself. "What do you know?"

Beth turned around as Rae quickly slipped into the pajamas, but when she bent over to pick up her slacks to give to her mom, Beth's eyes grew wide.

"Is that a fairy?" she asked curiously.

Rae's heart skipped a beat as she froze. Well...what was the harm? Might as well figure out what other latent memories her mom might still be carrying.

"Yeah, it is," she said brightly. She turned around and lifted her shirt, but kept a careful distance from Beth's hands. She didn't know what exactly was holding her back, especially because every fiber of her being was aching to reach out and touch her mother, but she somehow sensed that she should wait. When the time was right...she would know it.

"Wow," Beth remarked admiringly, "that's beautiful. The detail is exquisite." Then she gave Rae a speculative look. "When did you get it?"

"On the morning of my sixteenth birthday." Rae gulped and tried to act casual. "Do you have any ink?"

Beth chuckled softly. "Actually, I do. And it's in the exact same spot as yours. Oddly, with a bit of a similar pattern." She turned around and lifted up the back of her own shirt. Rae's eyes widened as she was finally able to see her mother's tatù for herself. It was absolutely spectacular—a swirling, looping, blinding sun. Rae could almost feel the heat coming off of it. It was closer to her own tatù than she had ever imagined, just with even more detail due to its size.

"That's amazing," she breathed. Again, she resisted the urge to touch her mother and turned instead to her quilted bed. She felt her fingers burn and quickly shoved them behind her back, afraid fire would shoot out of them. "Thank you again so much for letting us stay here tonight miss... I'm sorry, I actually never got your first name."

"It's Beth," her mother answered cheerfully, grabbing the little pile of Rae's clothes. "And yours?"

Rae had to take a quick, steadying breath before she could speak. "It's Rae."

"Rae?" Her mother frowned thoughtfully. "That's a *lovely* name. Does it run in your family?"

Unwelcome tears started pooling in Rae's eyes and she did her best to ignore them. "I honestly don't know. I never got a chance to ask my mom."

Beth smiled distractedly before gesturing to the bed. "Well goodnight. Hopefully you'll feel better after a good night's rest."

"Yes, thank you." Rae couldn't quite keep all the pain from her voice. "Good night."

The second the door closed behind Beth, Rae fell onto the bed in a mess of silent, hysterical tears. What had happened? How could her own mother not know her? What had they done to her!

She muffled her sobs in the quilt, vaguely aware that Devon was sure to be able to hear them, quartered in the living room directly below. Sure enough, after a few minutes, a soft whisper floated up through the floor boards.

"Rae, honey, are you all right?"

Rae pulled herself together with a shaky breath. "Yeah, I'm fine. Sorry to wake you."

"You didn't wake me." She could almost see his concerned eyes as he spoke. "Do you want me to sneak up there?"

She snorted. "I don't think that would be the best idea. I mean, you heard my mom. She and Carter would have a fit if they caught you."

Devon laughed softly. "Yeah. I can't believe I was actually banished to the couch by your mom. It seems so...normal, for us."

Rae shook her head with a smile. "Trust me. Nothing about this is normal."

"What're you going to do in the morning?" he asked quietly.

She sighed. "I'm not exactly sure."

But as she looked down at the tearstained quilt, a sudden idea popped into her head. She stroked the material with trembling fingers as a small smile began creeping up her face.

"I think I have a plan..."

The next morning, Rae woke up to the smell of bacon and scrambled eggs. Her clothes were sitting folded on a chair by the bed, and she put them on quickly before hurrying downstairs. Carter and Devon were already sitting at the table as her mother flew around the kitchen. Pouring some coffee here, prodding something on the grill over there. She was a blur of nervous energy.

"Good morning," she said brightly as Rae took a seat by Devon. "How would you like your eggs?"

"Uh," Rae glanced at the boys' plates and followed suit. "Scrambled is fine. Thank you."

With a grand relish, Beth tilted some eggs onto her plate and watched as she took the first, steaming bite. Rae's throat closed up automatically to protect itself and she struggled to keep a smile plastered on her face. It was like biting into the bottom of a dumpster.

"S'good!" she choked, with her mouth still full.

Beth turned around with a satisfied smile and Rae quickly spit them into her napkin. She cast a tortured glance at Devon only to see him smirking back at her, shaking his head as he poured some of his into a crack in the floor. Only Carter was immune—gobbling them down and staring at Beth like her cooking was God's gift to the world.

When they'd finally finished—or pretended to finish—Rae stood up in a sudden rush. "Well, thank you so much again for breakfast, Beth, and for letting us stay. But we should really get going."

The men looked at her in confusion as Beth blinked quickly, caught off guard by the sudden rush. "Oh, okay, of course." She got slowly to her feet and stared around the sudden flurry in her kitchen as everyone gathered up their jackets and scarves. "Well, are you sure you don't want some more coffee?" she offered hopefully.

"Nope, we've got to hit the road," Rae answered. "Thanks again."

The three of them headed out the door and down the cobblestone path with Beth trailing along behind, staring after them in a daze. Without understanding why, Carter and Devon slid obediently into the car and started up the engine, while Rae turned around for a final wave. Beth was standing halfway up the walk, that same shadow clouding her lovely features.

"Bye, Beth," Rae called breathlessly, preparing to drive away from her long-lost mother, "thanks for everything." She paused for a moment, waiting, but Beth said nothing and she turned slowly back to the car.

It felt like a knife had been lodged in her ribs, keeping her heart from properly beating.

Come on, Mom, she thought. *I'm your daughter! You know me!*

Nothing happened.

In what felt like slow motion, Rae pulled open her door and began to climb inside.

"Wait!"

Rae whirled around to see Beth running after her. She froze beside the car as her mother took her by the arms and spun her around.

"Why did you call me mom?"

Rae's heart leapt as silent tears ran down her cheeks. It had been a gamble, but this is what she had been counting on. The only emotion strong enough to pull Beth back to them was the utter heartbreak you feel when you lose someone you love. It was a pain Rae had quietly lived with for the last twelve years. She knew exactly how powerful it was.

"Because your name is Bethany Kerrigan. You're the ex-wife of Simon Kerrigan. Your brother attended Guilder and when you turned sixteen, they realized you were marked instead of him, they sent him home. You joined the Privy Council in England. You're a fighter, a badass, and an honestly terrible cook." She stared straight into Bethany's lovely eyes, her chest heaving. "I know all that...because you're my mother."

There was a long pause as Bethany stared back at her in the brilliant sunrise. The first rays of light shone down on them, casting away the shadows and illuminating what had been dark just moments before.

"I am." Bethany didn't say it as a question, more like an affirmation of things she knew deep in her heart to be true. Rae's breath caught in her chest as her eyes brimmed over with emotion. In a rush of adrenaline, she pulled up the back of her shirt and showed her mother again the sparkling fairy dancing in a bed of suns on her back. Without Rae even having to think about it, a blinding array of blue flames sprang up from her hand and began travelling up her arm.

Beth gasped, but didn't pull away as Rae reached for her.

"And this," Rae took her mother's hand and watched as the flames spread harmlessly across both their bodies, uniting mother and daughter, "is not a tattoo."

Chapter 13

"I just don't understand." Silence followed a moment with shock. "She's been living in France this whole time?"

Rae glanced at her mother out of the corner of her eye. The four of them were in the car, driving as fast as they could back to London. While her mother hadn't remembered any other details about what had happened the day of the fire or how she had ended up in France, she completely accepted the fact that she was Rae's mother and that the lot of them apparently had superpowers. Even now in the car, she was rhythmically snapping her fingers, delighted when a tiny blue flame shot out of the end of them. Devon, sitting in the passenger seat directly in front of her, stroked the back of his hair nervously and looked decidedly less pleased.

"Rae! Rae, are you listening?"

Rae turned her attention back to her ecstatic, frantic uncle waiting on the phone.

"I'm sorry," she apologized. "Apparently, she's been living in France for over a decade. She has no idea how she got there or what happened all those years ago, but she recognizes me now." Rae grinned as her mother tossed a flame from one hand to another. "I think things are starting to come back." She pushed the phone away from her mouth. "Hey Mom? Be careful."

"Could you please not do that in the car?" Devon asked imploringly.

"Said the boy who tried to sleep in the same bed as my daughter," Beth shot back. She smiled but there was a steel beneath the honey.

Devon flushed beet red. "That was her idea—I didn't say a thing."

Beth raised her eyebrows. "Oh, now you want to *blame* my daughter? You think that's going to earn you points?"

"I'm never going to win here, am I?" he muttered.

"No, but I love that you keep trying." She chuckled and Devon shook his head, trying to hide an exasperated smile.

Rae kept glancing between them, grinning from ear to ear. She couldn't believe that all the things she loved most in the world were coming together in a freak sort of blissed-out heaven. She felt light as air, like she could skip across the golden clouds that were crisscrossing their way back to the Chunnel.

"Did she remember anything? That she has a brother?" Uncle Argyle asked eagerly.

"I told her she had an obsessive compulsive, neurotic little brother, if that's what you mean."

"Rae Kerrigan!" Uncle Argyle's Scottish accent rolled his r's in frustration.

Rae giggled into her hand. "I'm kidding! Of course I told her. She's really excited to meet you. *Again.*"

"Well, I'm hopping on the next plane to London. I just," he said and sighed. "I can't believe she's alive." His voice grew thick with emotion. "I could never accept the fact she had died, even after all this time. I just couldn't imagine a world without her." He cleared his throat briskly. "I've no idea what I'm going to tell your aunt!"

"Tell her...I don't know. Tell her she was in a coma. And...misplaced. In France."

It was Uncle Argyle's turn to laugh. "I think I'll have to come up with something better than that."

"Well you know what they say, if you want something done right, do it yourself."

"Isn't it my job to provide the proverb?"

Rae shrugged. "What can I say? I'm feeling unpredictable." Her voice grew thoughtful as she stared again at her mother. "Just get over here, please? We have about a million family dinners to start catching up on."

"Will do. Drive safe."

"And you fly safe."

He hung up and Rae glanced down at her phone. The first thing she'd done once they were in the car was dial her uncle, and only now was she seeing the massive amount of missed correspondence from various people in her life. It was a wonder her phone hadn't run out of memory. She smiled as she scrolled down, selecting a random one from Julian.

I just drew a picture of you somehow setting yourself on fire. Please explain.

She giggled as she typed a reply: **You need to pay closer attention to detail, my friend. Not me, my mother. And I wasn't setting her on fire...exactly. Headed back to London. Will explain everything then. ⊠**

After Julian's, there were about a dozen from Molly. They ranged from wild speculations that Rae's mother had been caught up in an underground French slave trade, to her firm belief that Carter had no doubt imprisoned Rae and Devon in some sort of tatù-proof dungeon for their insubordination. Rae read through them all, struggling to suppress her laughter as Molly's theories ranged from just mildly crazy to utterly ludicrous. Then she remembered that as far as Molly knew, she and Devon were still trying to get to France with Carter hot on their trail.

She was about to go into full detail and explain, when a sudden whimsy seized her and she ended up sending just one, happy message: **Guess who's coming to dinner?**

With Molly and Julian out of the way, the bulk of the messages were from an increasingly-concerned Jennifer. Rae bit her lip as she glanced through the frenzied texts. It looked like Jennifer had been going out of her mind with worry.

Instead of texting, Rae decided she needed to call her mentor. The woman had been her mom's best friend before everything had happened. She was going to be one of the key helpers in bringing her mom's memory back. She'd done missions with her mom and could fill her in on how much of a superstar her mom really was.

Jennifer answered on the first ring. "Tell me what's happening."

"We found her!"

There was a long pause during which all Rae could hear was rapid breathing. Finally, she frowned and clutched the phone closer to her ear.

"Hello? You okay Jennifer?"

"Yes, sorry. I'm here." Jennifer's voice sounded more subdued than Rae had ever heard it before. Almost childlike in its uncertainty. "So... How is she? What did she say when she saw you?"

Rae spoke gently, sympathetic to her mentor's shock. After all, it would be like getting Molly back after a decade of thinking she'd died. Rae honestly didn't know how she'd handle it. "That's the thing, she didn't remember me...at first."

"But then she did?" Jennifer's voice was sharper now, sounding more like herself.

"Sort of." Rae glanced again at Beth—staring out the window now as they neared the water. "She knows she's my mother, but she doesn't remember anything else. She doesn't know what happened to her or who she is. She didn't even know she had a tatù until I..." She tried to think of a way to explain what she'd done. "Until I activated it for her."

"Wait—you *activated* it?"

"It's a long story," Rae sighed. "The shortened version is that I set her on fire."

She thought about the words with a slight frown in the silence that followed. Yeah, it sounded pretty bad, and must have looked even worse. She could understand Julian's concern, and Jennifer's.

"Well," Jennifer still sounded tentative, "way to make a first impression. I guess you wouldn't have it any other way. Where're you guys now? Is Carter with you?"

"Yeah, he's here. We're on our way back to London. We'll meet you guys at the hospital." Rae's face clouded with concern and she turned to face the window. "How's Luke doing? Did he make it out of surgery okay?" After checking in with Julian and Molly, Rae couldn't believe she'd forgotten what had happened to Luke.

"Yes and no." It sounded like Jennifer was carefully editing herself. "He made it out of surgery, but... Rae, we should just wait until you get here."

"No! What happened?" All the blood drained from Rae's face. "Tell me now!"

Bethany glanced over at the sudden shift in tone and squeezed Rae's knee comfortingly.

"There was a complication during surgery," Jennifer replied slowly. "Too much swelling in his brain. They had to put him into a medically induced coma when they were finished to wait for it to go down and him to wake up."

Rae's breath caught in her chest. "And if he doesn't?"

Devon glanced at her from his dashboard mirror, fully capable of hearing both sides of the conversation.

"He will, Rae, don't worry." Jennifer tried to sound confident. "Give him some time, and he's going to wake up. I'm sure you'll be here when he does."

Devon nodded deliberately and Rae caught the action from the back of his head. Rae forced a smile. "Yeah, I'm sure he'll be fine."

"In the meantime, I'm going to book us all rooms at the hotel across the street," Jennifer said. "You're going to want to be close to your friend, they might want to try to figure out what's going on with Beth..." She sighed softly into the phone. "I just can't believe she's back. I wonder what happened."

"I don't know..." Rae said softly, cupping her hand over her mouth. She watched her mother bantering cheerfully back and forth with Devon and a fierce protective fire sprang up in her chest, clouding out every other emotion. "...but I think I know a way to find out."

After they got off the Chunnel, they stopped at a restaurant within sight of London. They needed to. One, being that none of them had eaten anything since Beth's egg-debacle that morning. Two, everyone felt the need to sit down and take a breath before hurtling back into the whirlwind of the city. And three, Bethany still had some rather important unanswered questions.

"So, just to be sure," she held her hands up carefully in front of her face, "this flame thing can't start without my permission, right? I'm not going to reach for the salt shaker and accidently set the whole table on fire?"

Rae giggled as Carter shook his head. He'd been looking in the review mirror all day and blinking, like he wasn't sure he was dreaming. He couldn't take his eyes off her mom. "No, it doesn't just happen on its own. You're in complete control. That being said, it might take some practice to get back to the level you were at before the...disappearance. It'll be like being sixteen all over again." He reached for her hand and gave it a squeeze. "I know you'll get there."

Beth nodded seriously before giving Carter a speculative look. She opened her mouth like she was going to say something, but after a short pause, she turned to Rae instead.

"When you three first showed up at my house yesterday," she gave Carter another almost nervous glance, "you said you were travelling with your dad..."

"Oh! No, no, no!"

Everyone was quick to reassure her.

"Carter's not your husband."

"I promise, Beth, we're not and were never married."

"Sorry, Mom," Rae chuckled, "I was just trying to think of a plausible story."

Beth nodded once and took a swig of her iced tea. "That's what I thought."

Carter set down his coffee with a soft thud. "What's that supposed to mean?" Beth stared at him blankly and he elaborated. "'That's what you thought?' Like it would be so inconceivable—"

Devon kicked him not so discreetly under the table. "Keep it together, man," he muttered.

Fortunately, at that moment their burgers arrived. No one said anything for a while as they dug in, suddenly aware of how hungry they actually were. It was incredible how much all of their worlds had changed in just the last twenty-four hours and the whiplash of it left them struggling to keep up.

"So, let me get this straight..." Beth finally set down an uneaten crisp and pushed back her chair. "I have superpowers," she glanced around the table, "we all have these ink abilities, and that's what the tattoo is on my back?"

"Tatù," the three of them corrected her automatically. "But yes," Devon added.

"Right." Beth nodded. "I married a man with a superpo—tatù—even though I wasn't supposed to and had an illegal love child." She smiled at Rae warmly and took her hand. "Things were good." Her eyes clouded as she tried to keep it all straight. "Until I realized my husband was crazy, then I joined up with a covert organization to start spying on him, and then I disappeared in the midst of a mysterious fire everyone assumed killed me."

Devon nodded cheerfully, pleased she was catching on so fast. "That about sums it up, yeah."

She shot him a look. "What I don't understand is why everyone thought I died in a fire when it's clear that fire can't hurt me."

Carter nodded understandingly. "At the time of your disappearance, your powers hadn't yet progressed to the point where fire could travel over your entire body. Or maybe you knew and never told anyone that was part of your ability. You see, you have a very unique tatù. There are some that are common, but yours, like Rae's, is very exceptional. It wasn't until Rae discovered the latent ability in herself that she realized the truth and started trying to find you," he explained, handing her another sugar. She looked at him blankly and his cheeks flushed. "I remember you like two in your tea..."

She took the sugar with a slight smile before turning her attention back to Rae. "So you have two abilities, mine and your father's?"

"Yep." Rae swallowed down a gulp of her milkshake, eager to impress. "I can control fire like you, but I can also mimic the abilities of others. I have a whole store of them. I didn't know I had your ability till not too long ago. I thought I only had Simon's."

Beth leaned forward, unable to keep the excitement from her face. "What kinds of things can you do?"

Devon, heads up! Rae warned him with her mind.

He'd just looked up in surprise when Rae lobbed half a crisp his way. It blurred through the air, almost too fast to follow, but his hand shot up and caught it without him looking.

Beth's mouth fell open as she stared in between the two. "That's incredible."

"Devon has heightened abilities," Rae explained. "Speed, hearing, agility. His is usually my go-to tatù."

"I didn't know that," Devon said with a smile.

Rae shrugged casually. "Of course."

"*Really.*" Beth shot him a suspicious look. "Well, I guess that makes sense. He's a boy who likes to move *fast.*"

"Am I ever going to live that down?" Devon threw his hands in the air. "It wasn't even me."

Both Beth and Rae broke into simultaneous laughter as Beth shook her head. "No, I'm afraid you won't. Mother's prerogative and all that."

"Fantastic," he teased sarcastically, "so good to have you back, Mrs. Kerrigan."

Beth chuckled again. "I'm glad to be here! To keep an eye on you two..."

A few minutes later, Beth and Rae were heading back to the car. Devon and Carter had lingered inside to pay and to give the two of them at least a few moments of time alone.

"There's actually something else I don't understand." Beth put her arm around Rae and lowered her voice. "Simon, your dad, and I weren't supposed to get married because it's not allowed for two tatùs to be in a relationship, right?"

What felt like a heavy stone settled in the pit of Rae's stomach. She had a good idea where her mother was going with this. "That's right..."

"So I have to ask." Beth stopped them walking and turned her daughter to face her. "What're you doing with Devon?"

Rae sighed. "It's complicated. Devon and I are..." How did she say it? How did she find the words to sum up what she and Devon were? "We're in love," she said simply. "He's the love of my life and we want to have a future together. Whether or not the Privy Council agrees. We'll figure it out as we go. We kind of just sort of admitted our feelings for each other. It's been a long bumpy road since I turned sixteen."

"I'm sorry. I should have been there."

Rae waved her hand. "It doesn't matter. You're here now."

Beth frowned with concern. "But how is that, your relationship, going to work?"

The door opened and closed and they looked up to see both men walking toward them. Rae sighed again as Devon flashed her a smile from across the lot. "I don't know. We're kind of figuring it out as we go."

Beth nodded thoughtfully before staring at Carter with a speculative, curious grin.

"So Carter and I really never—"

"Oh, come on, Mom," Rae cut her off and held up a hand in disgust, "like I need that image."

The ride back to London was a breeze, thanks in large part to the diplomatic flags Carter's car still had flapping. Rae sent a text to Molly when they were near to the hospital, and by the time they'd parked, a flash of crimson hair was streaking towards them from across the lot.

"Rae!" Molly collided with her and sent them both stumbling backwards. Rae easily corrected their balance with a tatù. "I'm so sorry about Carter," she exclaimed as she squeezed the life out of her. "I did my best to throw him off your trail." Her eyes flashed up and landed guiltily on Carter himself. "No offense, sir."

"None taken," Carter replied stiffly.

"Anyway, so much has been happening since you've been gone! Your mentor has launched a full-out investigation about..." She suddenly fell silent as her eyes fell on Beth. "Is this...?" Her eyes widened in amazement. "Are you my best friend's mom?"

Before Beth could answer, Molly jumped on her in an embrace just as tight as the one she'd been using to discreetly strangle Rae.

"Oh my goodness!" Beth squeaked out.

"It's so good to meet you!" Molly gushed. "I can't believe we haven't met sooner, but I guess that would've been impossible, seeing as everyone thought you were dead. I'm Molly, Rae's best friend. We met at Guilder. We were actually roommates our first year. Now, I work for the Privy Council just like Rae and Devon do, although my job is a bit more important. I'm a designer—"

"Molly!" Rae clamped her hands down on her friend's shoulders. "Take a breath."

"Is that her power?" Beth whispered to Devon. "Talking like that?"

Devon gave her a long-suffering sigh. "Nope. That's just Molly."

Beth chuckled softly in the background as Rae fixed her attention on Molly. "Now what're you talking about? Jennifer launched an inquiry?"

A shadow darkened Molly's sunny face. "She didn't tell you?"

A chill ran up Rae's spine—she rarely saw her friend so serious. "Tell me about what?"

"It's about Luke." Molly lowered her voice. "Apparently, a lot of his wounds look self-inflicted. When Jennifer went to check out the place he's been staying, it was spotless—like he'd been planning to go away."

Rae's brow furrowed up in confusion. "What does that even mean? She thinks he did it to himself?! When we found him, he was unconscious, bleeding a swimming pool onto the floor. She really thinks he'd do something like that to—"

"I have no idea what she thinks." Molly held up her hands innocently. "I'm just telling you what she said."

"Well, she's wrong." Rae felt Devon's hand slip into her own. "She has to be."

Molly nodded quickly. "I'm sure she is. She's just being thorough. She's trying to protect you, Rae. That's her job."

There was an awkward silence for a minute, before Carter cleared his throat. "I hate to break up this little reunion, but I'm heading back to Guilder to meet with the rest of the Council. We're going to need to figure out what to do about this...situation with Beth."

The hair on the back of Rae's neck bristled defensively. "What *situation* is that?"

"Her safety," Carter replied instantly, soothing Rae's fears. "We have no idea who attacked Beth on the day of the fire. We've no idea if they're still out there and if they're going to try again." His eyes softened tenderly as they fell on Beth's face. "We need to protect her."

Devon nodded seriously. "Rae and I will cover that while you're gone. Nothing will happen to her, I swear."

"I know," Carter said. "She's in safe hands and Rae isn't going to let this one out of her sight. Jennifer will also be right beside you."

"We all will." Rae chewed her lip a moment. "Carter, do you think Lanford's responsible? He fooled me, fooled all of us. He'd been playing his cards until he could get me. I bet money that he's the one who did this to my mom. See if you can find out anything there first." Rae squeezed his hand and waved goodbye as Carter made his leave and took off back out of the parking lot. Once he was gone, the three of them headed inside.

Rae's head was a mess of different emotions. On the one hand, she had never been happier in her life. Her mother was back from the dead. Everything was going to be different now. Better. Rae was going to have a family—a *slightly* more normal life. However, on the other hand, Luke lay in a coma just behind these doors. What was more, Rae's very own mentor, a person she'd come to trust in spite of all her defenses, suspected him of foul play. Could Luke be involved in something dangerous? Or some kind of cover up?

She was still trying to make sense of it all as they breezed through the double doors and found Jennifer standing there at attention. Jennifer's eyes grew wide as they fell on Beth, but it wasn't her that spoke. In fact, it wasn't Molly or Rae or anyone else who could make an introduction.

"I can't believe it."

Everyone turned at the same time to where Rae's mother stood frozen in the doorway.

Beth's mouth fell open as she took half a step forward. "Jenn?"

Chapter 14

"Wait a minute..." Rae felt the excitement rising up in her chest. "You remember her?!"

It was coming back! Her mother's memory was really coming back!

Jennifer took a step backwards into the nurse's counter, watching Beth's every move with an almost cautious look in her eye. Clumsy with shock. She'd thought her best friend was dead, over a decade ago and it was probably like seeing a ghost.

For her part, Beth seemed merely confused. "I-I think I do." She gave Jennifer a tentative smile. "We were friends back at the Privy Council, weren't we? We went on... missions together?"

"That's right." Jennifer's face cleared, but her voice shook with emotion. "You were my best friend—we did everything together. I met you just after I turned sixteen."

"Oh my goodness, this is so cute!" Molly leaned over and whispered to Rae. "It's like how you and I would be if one of us got amnesia." Her eyes travelled briefly over Beth's house clothes to Jennifer's signature badass leather. "I'd be Jennifer," she concluded decisively.

Rae rolled her eyes and took a step towards her mom. She put her hand on Beth's elbow as if to guide her back through time. "Her name is Jennifer Jones—her tatù is a leopard. You two used to work together from what I heard. On some badass missions. I believe you and her were deep undercover trying to catch Dad." When her mom looked more confused, Rae tried a slightly different approach. "She was helping you gather information to take down Simon Kerrigan."

Jennifer's head jerked as if she'd been slapped. "And look where that got us," she murmured. As she stared at Beth, her eyes glistened with unshed tears.

"When I was nearly finished with school at Guilder, I joined up with the PCs, Jennifer came back specifically to work as my Botcher."

Beth's eyebrows rose. "Botcher?"

Rae waved her hand, half rolling her eyes. "It's an old Tudor term the PC's use. I'm a Dagonet, and Jenn's my Botcher. A Botcher back in King Henry's time was a mender of old clothes. Apparently it's a secret term used back then to hide the trainer of tatù people when the whole school and Privy Council started. Their job was to fix and mend tatù abilities to perfection. A Dagonet, ironically, refers to a foolish young knight. Someone who simply thinks their armor—or tatù—makes them strong and forgets to think or use it properly."

Her mom stared at her like she was crazy.

Rae laughed. "So basically Jenn's my mentor. She's supposed to help train me and keep an eye out for me in the field. Which she's done, more than once." She winked at Jennifer. "Thanks. In case I forgot to say it. Thanks for saving my arse more than once."

"Is that right?" Beth answered softly. She crossed the hall of the lobby and came to a stop directly in front of Jennifer, giving her nowhere else to look. "You did that?"

Jennifer's eyes flew wildly around the room as she let out a bark of laughter. "I can't believe I'm standing here talking to you right now." She seemed to be having trouble keeping Beth in focus, as if looking at her brought forth too much pain.

Beth stood undeterred. "You looked after my girl for me?" she pressed again.

Jennifer's face tightened. "I did. I had to. She was yours—"

The next second, Beth had Jennifer in her arms. A look of complete shock paled Jennifer's face as Beth squeezed her tight. "Thank you," she said simply.

"Any time," Jennifer gasped.

Molly swooned again and even Rae had to admit it was almost funny. Jennifer was the hardest, most guarded person she had ever met. Not exactly prone to fits of hugging and deep emotional reunions. It looked like she honestly didn't know what to do with all the love.

Eventually, she pried Beth's hands loose and wriggled free. "So you really remember nothing about the fire?" she asked seriously, searching Beth's eyes. "You have no idea who did this to you?"

"No." Beth shook her head. "I keep trying, but no. I don't remember a thing."

Jennifer's eyes burned with rage. "We'll find out," she swore. "We're going to find out exactly who did this and I'm going to hold them personally responsible." She gritted her teeth together, but as she stared back at Beth, her face slowly crumbled. "Beth, you have to know... You and Simon...the fire...? Nothing went according to plan." She hung her head in remorse and shivered as Bethany hugged her again.

"I know." She patted Jennifer's back sympathetically. "I volunteered to spy. I knew the risks. There was nothing you could have done."

When Jennifer said nothing, Rae stepped forward. "You can't blame yourself," she volunteered softly, "you taught me that. It was beyond your control."

Jennifer pulled away again and shot Rae a peculiar look. Rae blushed and stepped back. She guessed that Jennifer would never in a million years blame herself for a mission gone bad. This was hate and revenge, not regret she was feeling.

"Or..." Rae amended quickly. "We could just hunt them down and kick some arse. Make things right."

For the first time, the corner of Jennifer's mouth twitched up. "*That*...sounds like a plan."

Beth tilted suddenly and both Rae and Jennifer reached out to steady her.

She held her hand up to her head and offered the two of them a shaky smile. "I for one might need to get a little rest before we charge into battle. Using that tatù for the first time really took it out of me and..." She stroked the side of Rae's face with a soft smile. "I feel like my world's still spinning."

Rae nodded quickly. "Absolutely." She wanted to check in on Luke but felt hesitant to say it. She looked at Devon, who had stood off to the side watching the interaction.

"Why don't you take your mom to the hotel I set up for us? It saves heading to Heath Hall."

Rae stared out the window and then pointed across the street. "Is that the one?"

"I believe so. Carter booked a block of rooms when we arrived the other day." She looked at Beth with a worried frown, hesitant to let her go. "Why don't I come with you? Make sure you settle in okay?"

Devon stepped forward. "Why don't we let these two have some time alone? Mother-daughter time," he suggested. "Beth'll be fine with Rae, and they're right across the street if they need anything. Rae," he said and tapped his temple, "can get a hold of me here if there's an emergency. Which there won't be." He turned back to Jennifer. "Or she can call us if she needs one of us."

A rush of gratitude welled up in Rae's chest and she smiled warmly. "But what'll you do?"

"I'm going to stay with Luke," he said automatically. "Sit with him in case he wakes up."

Molly raised her eyebrows in amazement, but Rae simply nodded. She was bowled over by the generosity of his actions, but not all that surprised. Devon was one of the good guys. One of the best. She would expect nothing less.

"Thank you," she said sincerely before turning back to Beth. "Come on, Mom, let's go rack up Carter's room-service tab."

"Are you sure you don't want me to come with you?" Jennifer asked in a rush. "Keep an eye out for anything out of the ordinary?"

Beth laughed. "This whole thing is out of the ordinary. We'll be fine, Jenn."

Jenn had just found her best friend, she didn't seem ready to let her go. "I can stand outside your room and guard it."

Rae smiled. "I appreciate the offer but I think I can protect my mom right now. I have been taught by the best."

Beth grinned. "And if memory serves, I can take care of myself."

The group chuckled as she and Rae walked back outside and headed to the hotel. When they were across the street, Beth leaned over and said, "But it doesn't serve—not at all. How can I not remember *anything* that happened the day I lost everything?"

"Don't worry about that," Rae said with a faint grin. "I've come up with a bit of a plan..."

"Say again?" Beth asked with a slightly disturbed frown. "You're going to *probe* my mind?"

"For Pete's sake, Mom, anyone can hear you." Rae bolted up off the bed and shut the curtains on the window. They were on the ground floor and people were wandering casually in and out of the parking lot just beyond. "It's not as bad as it sounds," she continued. "I'm not going to *probe your mind*, I'm going to search your memories. One memory in particular."

"The day of the fire," Beth finished.

Rae nodded. "That's the idea. Curtis' power doesn't let me change the past—not really—but I can see it and re-live it just like I was standing there."

Beth frowned. "Is it dangerous for you?"

"I don't think so," Rae shrugged casually. "After all, my body stays right here. It's more like a shared trip down memory lane." She said it with confidence, but Beth got up and began pacing.

"I don't know, sweetie. There are a lot of variables to consider."

Rae threw up her hands. "Like what?"

"Like who the other body was," Beth said seriously. "You said they discovered two bodies in the fire, and contrary to popular opinion, I can say with complete certainty that one of them wasn't me. That means I didn't burn up in the fire that killed me and my husband, someone else was there. Probably the same person who smuggled me off to France." She took Rae firmly by the shoulders. "The same person that let two people die." A crease formed in the center of her forehead and she dropped her fierce gaze. "Not to mention, no matter how bad he was, I don't think I want to send you back in time so you can watch your own father die."

Rae hadn't considered that, and for a moment, she froze. How would it feel to see the burning corpse of her dad? Would she feel satisfaction? Relief, even, that he was removed so quickly from her young life? No. Despite her misgivings, she didn't think she was that heartless. When he died that day, a part of her died as well. He was her dad, after all. Crazy or not, he was still family.

But who killed him? Who was lying beside him as he burned? Who was the mystery person who got Beth out of the house? Was it Simon's own brainwashing device that was used to erase his wife's memory? Why had Beth been taken while Rae was left behind?

All these questions needed answers. And now, for the first time in her life, Rae finally had the chance to find them. "I don't care." She tilted her chin upwards and looked her mother straight in the eye. "I want to do it, Mom. We deserve to know what happened that day. To *both* of us."

That caught Beth off guard and she took a step back. She frowned for a moment, studying Rae carefully, before slowly inclining her head. "You're right," she acquiesced. "We both need some answers."

"Really?" Rae exclaimed, unable to believe her luck. She had been prepared to argue it out for the next hour or so.

"Really," Beth said firmly. "So how do we do this?"

"I'll show you," Rae said eagerly.

Beth chuckled. "No, baby girl. I guess *I'll* be showing *you*."

They stood in the center of the room and held hands. At Rae's prompting, Beth closed her eyes and let her mind go blank, clearing the way for Rae to search for the memory. When it looked like Beth was relaxed, Rae took a deep breath and dove inside.

It was unlike anything she'd experienced before—completely different from the times she'd used it on Philip and Devon. Instead of sinking down into a blur of colors and sounds, the world around her was blank. Completely void of anything to stimulate the senses.

For a moment, Rae stared into the gray nothingness with rising panic. What if she couldn't get back out again? She remembered this was the same premise that Curtis was using to help Maria remember who she was. If he could do it, so could Rae.

Squeezing her eyes shut, Rae tried to draw from any memories she herself had of the day, any detail that could help bring the image to light. She remembered the faded yellow paint on the wall by the calendar; the sweet, spent smell of withering roses in a crystal vase. She could see her mother there, smiling nervously as she prompted Rae to go outside. Rae remembered the checkered sundress she'd been wearing.

Then, all at once, the world around her was lit with color. Just like the fire inside her had sparked her mother's tatù—her memories had activated her mother's as well.

When she opened her eyes, Rae was standing in her old childhood kitchen. The day was exactly as she had remembered it. Sunny and warm, but with a hint of a breeze. The house looked warm as well, lived-in. Neat, but covered in scattered toys and finger-paintings pinned to the wall.

Rae had just reached out to touch a picture of a ladybug, when a person ran into the room, and her heart almost stopped in her chest.

"But Mommy, I don't want to go outside!" the little girl complained.

Her messy, raven curls had been held at bay with a headband and there were huge grass stains on her white tights. Her lower lip trembled with the injustice of being sent away and when she threw up her tiny hands in exasperation, Rae saw paint from the ladybug still under her little nails.

That's me, Rae thought with a silent gasp. *Twelve years ago.*

Then the reality of the situation smacked her in the face and her heart started beating double time.

I've got to get out of here!

Using Jennifer's tatù for speed, Rae blurred through the kitchen and crouched down behind the counter, silently panting for breath.

How could she have been so stupid? This wasn't going to work if little Rae grew up with a memory of big Rae in the kitchen with her the day of the fire. She might grow to believe she'd started it herself! What kind of guilty, suicidal feelings would that be sure to cause?!

Mind racing, Rae scrambled to see if she felt any belated guilt for the death of her parents. But before she'd gotten very far, another set of footsteps walked into the kitchen. Rae watched the shadow of two long legs come to a stop in front of the little girl, and when she was sure it was safe, she peeked the tops of her eyes out from her hiding spot.

It was her mother. Bent over Rae's past self with a smile. A smile that teenage Rae saw through quickly to the panic beneath, but little Rae thought was absolutely fine.

"You have to go out, sweetheart. Mommy needs to have some grownup time to talk to Daddy. You go enjoy the sunshine. Take your new markers and paper. Why don't you draw me a pretty picture?"

"But I don't *want* to," little Rae complained. "I could be a grownup. Can't I stay inside and have grownup time too? Remember, you said I was very mature for my age..."

Her mother laughed softly but shook her head. "Always the little bargainer. Tell you what, after I've talked to your father, I'll take you to the park for some ice cream. How does that sound?"

Rae's little face brightened in glee. "Perfect!" she squealed, bounding out the door. "I'll be in my treehouse."

Beth watched her go with a sad look on her face, knowing things and fearing things that her blissful little daughter did not. With a deep sigh, she shut the door to the yard silently behind her.

"I love you," she whispered to no one but herself.

Rae watched with tears in her eyes as her mother stared out into the yard, jumping in fright when a door slammed somewhere behind them.

"Beth? Where the hell are you?!"

Rae jumped as well as she recognized the voice of her father. She would have known it even if she hadn't been forced to sit through his indoctrination video just a few years prior. The angry, volatile tone had been burned into her mind years before.

"I'm in here," her mother replied. Beth spoke calmly, but there was a fire beneath the surface, as real as the sun burning on her back. "Just waiting for you, honey..."

In a rush of air, Simon Kerrigan swept into the room.

Rae's mouth dropped to the floor when she saw her father. While she had remembered her mother's face with perfect clarity, her father's had always been a bit of a blur. Fuzzy mouth, disjointed eyes—she could never quite piece together the entire puzzle. Looking at him now, she was glad she'd forgot. He strode forward and she crouched further behind the counter.

"You'll never guess who came to see me today," Simon raged.

Beth sighed wearily. "Who?"

"Jonathon Carter! He and the rest of the Council seem to think I'm building some mysterious weapon to use against them. It was all I could do to get away!"

Beth's eyes flashed but she smiled calmly. "And you think I have something to do with it?"

All at once, Simon grabbed her arms. "Don't play dumb with me Beth! I've known there's been a spy in my organization for years. I've run through everyone except one person."

"How could you even consider?"

"That my wife is a traitor?" He shook his head. "I trusted you. I loved you! You were all I wanted since the first time I met you! I tried to convince you about what you and I could do. The powers we could create! But no, you refuse to have more than Rae. You stupid whore, I need a boy! I want more!"

"That must make you so frustrated, sweetie." She put her hands lovingly on top of his, but he pulled them away with a yelp—nursing a burn. "Now keep your voice down. Rae's playing in the yard. Don't hurt her feelings." She must have believed he would never touch Rae. He had no idea what her ability was yet.

Simon got right up in her face and sneered. "I should just throw her in the car and take her with me. She'd be better off—better off with people who will appreciate her talents."

Beth brought herself up to her full height. "I'd like to see you try."

Simon raised up his hands and a sudden gust of wind knocked Beth back a few steps. Rae looked on in horror, but when Beth straightened up, she was laughing.

"Really? You come to fight *me* and that's the best you got? *David's* power?"

Simon snarled as another gale-force gust of wind stirred the air. Rae's nose wrinkled up as it blew her way. Was that smoke? Impossible. Her mother was standing right here. She must just be imagining it.

But Beth smelled it too. "Is something burning?" She frowned out towards the yard, and for a moment, Simon followed her gaze.

"It's probably just the Padgetts having another barbeque." The surprisingly banal domesticity of the answer surprised Rae. "Or it could be my scorched flesh," he finished.

Yeah, that was more like it.

He straightened up until all six foot two of him was baring down upon her. "Of all the people to betray me, Beth. Why did you do it?"

"Why did *you* do it?" she countered fiercely. "Why did you decide to put your crazed delusions of power in front of your family? You never wanted more children so we could be a family! You want a house full of scientific experiments! Little lab rats running about. Honestly Simon, you left me no choice."

"Delusions of power?" he yelled. "Beth, we have the ability to have more power than you could possibly imagine. When Rae turns sixteen—"

"*You leave her out of this!*" For the first time, Beth raised her voice. "I'll kill you myself before I let you lay a hand on our daughter!"

"Is that right?" Simon's eyes gleamed as he took a step forward. "Well if you insist..."

Rae's hand flew up over her mouth. She couldn't believe what she was hearing. She couldn't believe what she was seeing. It was getting harder and harder to breathe. Her skin was dripping with sweat and it was only seventy degrees outside.

Before she saw her father and mother actually come to blows, the front door slammed again. Both Beth and Simon froze in their tracks and stared at each other.

"Did Carter follow you back here or—"

It wasn't Carter who stormed into the kitchen. It was a woman Rae had never seen before, yet she suddenly had a good idea who she was. Tall, curly brown hair, and a cocky strut about her, even when she was standing still.

This had to be Kraigan's mother.

"I knew I'd find you back here," she shrieked at Simon before pointing a finger at Beth. "I knew you'd go running back to *her*!"

Beth's eyebrows shot up. "Excuse me? Simon, who the hell is this?"

The angry woman leaned around Simon and jabbed a finger in Beth's direction. "I'm the love of his life and the mother of his child. Who the hell are you?!"

Rae couldn't tell if the roaring in her ears was real or if it was all in her head.

For a second, Beth looked utterly astonished, gazing between her husband and the furious woman standing in her kitchen. Then her face broke into a huge laugh. "You have *got* to be kidding me!" She wiped hysterical tears from her face. "Of course you are. Well lady, he's all yours."

"Beth!" Simon held up his hand to stop her as she headed out to the yard. The temperature in the room seemed to be rising and he wiped a drip of sweat from his forehead. "I love you, Beth. Always have. This woman means nothing. It's for the greater good—"

"The greater good?!" Beth coughed in the thick air. "A woman shows up here claiming to have your love-child and you say it's for the greater—"

Before she could finish, there was a mighty crash as the beams in the ceiling above them suddenly gave way. Beth screamed as what looked like a wave of fire poured down from the upstairs, instantly covering the floor and snaking up the walls of the kitchen. Molten pieces of drywall and wood covered the ground, and Beth ran automatically forward, pulling pieces of rubble off the heap.

"Simon!" she shrieked, throwing aside huge chunks of the ceiling as she looked for him. She didn't seem to realize that she was on fire. "Simon, can you hear me?!"

Smoky tears stung Rae's eyes and she actually got to her feet, watching in horror as her mother desperately tried to dig her dead husband out of the burning rubble. Beth screamed and screamed until her voice grew hoarse, crying hysterically as the flames began to spread across her skin. Despite every red warning light flashing in her head, Rae was on the verge of running forward and helping her, when she suddenly realized they weren't alone.

A deathly chill ran up her spine and she had the good sense to drop back behind the counter before the intruder spotted her.

Jennifer! Jennifer? What the hell?

"Jennifer?" Beth shrieked, confirming Rae's fright. "What're you doing here?"

Jennifer stared at the flames consuming her friend's body and her mouth fell open in slow shock. But then another chunk of the second story fell into the first and she looked at the pile of burning debris in horror.

"Simon!" she screeched. "NO!"

She began digging furiously through the wreckage, not stopping until she pulled a bloody torso from the heap. With soot and tears streaking her face, Jennifer kissed Simon Kerrigan's lifeless lips as the house burned down around them.

Beth watched them, pale as a sheet, before she finally forced herself to speak.

"What're you doing?"

Jennifer snarled up at her like the leopard she was. "What are *you* doing *alive*?!" she screamed. "All of this was meant for you!"

The rest of the color drained from Beth's face. "It was you. You're the one that's been leaking secrets from the Privy Council. This whole time...it's been you."

Oblivious to the fact that she now had flames snaking up one side of her body, Jennifer leaned down for a final kiss before lying Simon gently on the floor. Then she stood up and patted out the flames on her leg with a dangerous calm.

"Yes, it's been me." She looked up at Beth with sheer murder in her eyes. "And you, Bethany Kerrigan, are never going to leave this house alive."

Unable to watch any more, Rae ripped open her eyes and stared back at her mother in the hotel room. Mirrored tears ran down both of their faces as they stood there, clutching each other's hands. It was as if the world around them was still burning. How could it be true?

Before Rae had a chance to say anything, there was a sudden thud. She watched in frozen confusion as her mother's eyes closed and she fell noiselessly to the floor. When Rae looked back up, Jennifer was standing in her place.

"So..." Her old mentor dropped the bloody telephone she'd used to bash against Beth's head. "I guess I have a lot of explaining to do."

Chapter 15

Rae couldn't speak. Couldn't think. Couldn't believe this was happening all over again.

Lanford...Kraigan...*Jennifer*?

What had she been thinking, opening herself up to such vulnerability *again*?! It was starting to be like clockwork. She would get close to a person, just to be betrayed. Close enough to see them smile as they pulled out the knife and stabbed it into her back. Or hit her over the head.

She dropped to her knees in terror and knelt beside her mom's crumpled form. "Mom? *Mom*!"

Her heart seized as she watched a small trickle of blood run through Beth's curls and pool on the floor. This couldn't be happening—not again! She could not have resurrected her mother only to watch her die...*again*!

A feral scream ripped through her teeth as she glared up at her ex-Botcher, standing calmly above them. "What did you *do*?!"

Jennifer was about to respond when Rae hit her with a bolt of electricity, sending her flying back into the far wall.

"You son of a bitch!" It didn't matter. Whatever Jenn was going to say didn't matter. Rae was going to lose her mom all over again because she'd opened them both up to someone she was stupid enough to trust.

The pool of blood grew steadily wider and Beth stirred with a faint moan. Feeling electrified herself, Rae reached around on the floor to snatch up her bloody phone, only to find out it had shattered upon impact with her mother's skull. Already sensing the outcome, Rae reached anyways for the hotel phone. The cord had been cut and the line was disconnected.

"You didn't think it would be that easy, did you?"

Rae straightened and rotated slowly around. In the last few years, she'd stared down her own death, the death of her friends, and the resurgence of her homicidal father's crazy cult. But she had never, in all that time, been as angry as she was right now. She stared at Beth, bleeding on the ground in between them, before she raised her eyes slowly to Jennifer. "I really don't think you want to be trapped in a room with me right now."

Jennifer threw back her head and laughed. "Oh! The kitty wants to play! All grown up now, are you, Rae? You forget—I know exactly how much training you have. I know all of your tatùs and I know exactly what each one can do." She smiled with mock sympathy. "I'm afraid you just don't have any tricks left up your sleeve."

Rae sent another bolt of electricity flying her way, but Jennifer dodged it with ease.

"In a way, you have no one to blame here but yourself," Jennifer said quietly and authoritatively as she took a step towards Rae and Bethany. "What was the first lesson I ever taught you? Above all the others?"

Rae stayed defiantly silent, and in the next second, she was flying through the air—cracking her head against the wall and sliding to the floor with a muffled groan. Something warm sprayed down the side of her face, and when she pulled back her hand, it was red with blood.

"You need to always be ready." Jennifer's voice cut through the air. "Get up." She snorted. "I taught you better than that."

Rae pulled herself to her feet and glared with all her might, ignoring the steady drip of blood running down her arm. "Why did you even bother?" she hissed. "If all this time, all you wanted to do was kill me."

That same peculiar look shadowed across Jennifer's face, before she shook her head with sudden determination. "It wasn't the plan to kill you." She gestured to Beth's motionless form. "Or her, for that matter. As long as she was out of the way, she didn't matter. But you had to go and find the bitch and now that you've brought her back there's a chance we could be exposed." She shrugged. "Well, the rules change."

We? Who was *we*?

Rae sucked in a breath and struggled to rein in her anger. Jennifer was right, this was no different from any other mission. Only in this case, she needed to get information that wasn't part of protocol. The only way to do that was to touch Jennifer's skin.

With a roar of rage, she launched herself with blinding speed across the hotel room, only to be immediately diverted by Jennifer's ready hands. She flew into the other wall this time and fell to the floor with a sickening crunch. The sound of Jennifer's laughter brought her back to her senses.

"Come on! My own tatù?! Show a little respect, would you?" She shook her head as she yanked Rae up to her feet, holding her by the hair as she dragged her to the center of the room. "It's like all this time I've been talking to a brick wall."

But beneath Jennifer's death grip, Rae smiled as she quickly healed herself with Charles' tatù. This sort of close proximity was exactly what she'd had in mind. Using Julian's tatù to predict Jennifer's next few movements, Rae rocketed up above their heads and brought Jennifer down to the floor, landing squarely on her chest. Jennifer gazed up at her in shock, but before she could fully recover, Rae ripped off her leather jacket and tossed it away.

She barely had time to marvel at the torn, burned skin beneath. The fire, she recalled. The flames had spread up one entire side of Jennifer's body. No wonder she always hid in this leather suit—the body below was ravaged beyond repair. It wasn't like she could tell anyone how she got the burns.

Without stopping to think, Rae seized Jennifer's shoulder in an iron grip, closing her eyes as her body automatically switched tatùs. The next second, she was back in the living room in Heath

Hall, watching as Jennifer crept up behind Luke and bashed him over the head.

There was a scream of rage as Jennifer tried to throw her off. However, Rae wasn't finished.

She picked up the same phone Jennifer had used to strike her mother, and smashed her across the face with it. Then she grabbed her by the neck and closed her eyes once more.

This time, she was back in her burning childhood home. The memory had picked up right where Beth's had left off. As Beth sprinted to grab Rae from the yard, Jennifer knocked her unconscious, using her tatù to bring her to the ground. Rae watched in horror as Jennifer knelt over her mother's unconscious body, ready to finish the job, but a deep, male voice floated down from nowhere and stopped her.

"Now, now, Miss Jones. That's not what we discussed."

Rae whirled around in surprise as a tall man with dark, trimmed curls walked slowly into the burning building. He didn't seem to notice the walls crumbling down around him—he only had eyes for Beth.

"She was never allowed to die, not when she could still be useful."

As screams from the neighbors and the faint sounds of sirens began welling up outside, Jennifer cast a panicked look to the backyard. "Her child, Simon's child is still out there."

The man shook his head. "The child is going to be collected by the authorities and sent to live with her uncle. She'll come to Guilder in time, and Guilder will open its doors to let her in."

Jennifer's teeth locked together in rage. "Then why do we need her?" She glared down at Beth with unmistakable hatred. "She did her part, she's had a purebred baby. Her job here is done."

For the first time, the strange man chuckled. "Such rage in you." He glanced down at Jennifer's flat stomach with a faint smile. "You'd think you were taking this personally."

Jennifer cried out in anguish and raised her hand up over Beth's head, but the man stopped her with a single word.

"Enough." He adjusted the cuffs on his jacket, suddenly bored with the conversation.

"We'll use her to test the limits of Simon's device. Stash her away and check on her throughout the years to make sure nothing ever comes back."

Jennifer was panting with silent tears, but she nodded her head and lifted Beth slowly from the ashes. "What if her daughter comes looking for her?"

"It's funny you should ask..."

Rae's heart froze in her chest as the man turned deliberately towards the counter. She didn't have time to run, she didn't have time to hide. She just stared up in horror as the man looked her right in the eye.

"I'm counting on it."

The characters blurred out as the room around them dimmed to black. Rae tried to pull out of the memory as Jennifer struggled and kicked beneath her, breaking her focus as she clawed Rae's bloody arm. Rae cried out in pain, but before she could pull out of Jennifer's mind entirely, a power beyond both their control took her to one more scene.

This one couldn't have been more different from the last. Rae blinked in confusion and tried to get her bearings in the bright, fluorescent light. They were in an office building of some kind, a doctor's office by the looks of it. Just her, Jennifer, Simon...and the baby in Jennifer's belly.

Rae's mouth fell open in silent shock, and she backed quickly into the changing room in the corner, relieved beyond belief that Jennifer was already wearing a hospital gown.

"I don't want to do this," a quiet voice almost whispered. There was such pain in the words, such unspeakable sadness, that Rae had to double check to make sure it was Jennifer who'd said it.

Sure enough, Jennifer was perched on the exam table, cradling her swollen abdomen with a thousand tears in her eyes. Rae had never seen her Botcher look so vulnerable, so small.

She looked up at Simon, pleading as the tears started to fall. "I can't—please. Don't ask me to do this..."

Simon stroked back her hair. It was an automatic gesture, brought about by habit and necessity, not feeling. "I'm afraid we have no choice," he said without inflection. "You heard the doctor, it's a girl. I have no need for another girl. I need a son."

Jennifer stifled a sob. "But why do we have to get rid of her? Why couldn't I just keep her in secret? No one would have to know—"

"Because we can't take the risk." Simon stroked her hair again, but his eyes were cold. "We can't have anyone figuring out what we're doing. I can't risk the ability getting passed on." She sobbed again and he made an impatient shushing sound. "Please, enough. We'll try again. We'll keep trying until I get what we need..."

The scene blurred and Rae came to in the hotel room. The front of her own shirt was wet with tears, and when she looked down, Jennifer was frozen beneath her, staring up with wide eyes.

"I didn't know..." Rae whispered. "I had no idea." She tasted the hit almost before she felt it. A rush of blood filled her mouth as she flew backwards through the glass window, landing in the broken shards in the parking lot. She spat out the blood and gasped for air as Jennifer jumped out the window after her. A defensive spray of electricity shot into the air between them as Rae tried to get up, but a sliver of glass had wedged itself deep under her shoulder blade and she couldn't seem to move.

"You bitch," Jennifer murmured as she stood above her, watching her struggle. She pressed her stilettoed boot down on a gash on Rae's leg and Rae tried not to scream. "*That* memory wasn't for you. *That* was supposed to be for *me*."

She kicked Rae hard in the ribs, and this time, Rae released a horrified, painful scream.

"After all," Jennifer continued, "since you came around, the only thing I got to keep of my baby was the memory of it. No need for another daughter—not when she might inherit the tatù instead of the son."

Rae reached behind her and pulled out the glass as she panted in pain. According to Alecia's tatù, it had missed most of the major arteries, but in the process, it nicked one of her lungs. She switched quickly to Charles' tatù to heal herself, but before she could, Jennifer crouched on top of her and punched her with impossible force in the face.

Rae felt her nose crunch in, and despite her need to stop the bleeding, her body switched defensively back to Molly's tatù, sending Jennifer flying back to her feet with a shower of sky blue sparks.

"Pretty weak voltage," Jennifer commented matter-a-factly, as calm as if they were back in the Oratory, practicing with sticks. "You must be losing quite a bit of blood. As much as your mom is inside."

"If you hurt her, I'll—"

"You'll what?" Jennifer interrupted her. "You've done exactly what I thought you would, Rae. You got emotional, got distracted. Couldn't keep your eyes on the prize. Your mother had the exact same problem—that inescapable need to feel. It's how I was able to get the drop on her the day of the fire. She was running out to the yard to save you."

Rae's face twisted in pain as she tried again to get up, but Jennifer kicked her back down with a triumphant grin.

"I guess I really was the stronger fit, the better partner for Simon. After all, I'm about to finish off his entire family, and I don't have so much as a scratch."

There was a flash of blinding light, and the next second, Jennifer was on the ground.

"You wanna bet, you two-timing-mommy-snatching-witch?"

"Mom!" Rae gasped and pulled herself up to a sitting position, waiting for Charles' tatù to take effect. "Mom, be careful, she—"

But Beth smiled. "Don't worry, sweetie." She looked down at Jennifer and her face grew cold. "I've got this."

Jennifer staggered to her feet and spat out a mouthful of blood. "So this is how it's going to end, is it? You or me?" She lowered her head slightly and Rae could practically feel the energy growing in her ready muscles. "You know what?" She grinned wickedly. "I actually prefer it this way."

Rae looked on in terror, but Beth chuckled softly. "Oh Jenn, you never got it, did you? I was always better. That's why Simon chose me. That's why the Privy Council chose me. That's why I'm coming back to a world full of family, friends. While you're going to die with nothing."

Jennifer growled and started to leap forward, but Beth shot her back to the ground with a wave of scorching hot fire. Rae could feel the heat of it travelling through the cement as Beth walked slowly forwards, blue flames flickering from her hands. It looked like her mom had finally gotten her whole tatù back.

"Doesn't matter if you kill me," Jennifer murmured, rolling back onto her feet and nursing a huge burn on the side of her face. "I'm not the only bad guy here. I'm only doing what I'm told."

Beth looked at her carefully, but in the end, she simply shook her head. "You're bad enough for me." Then she lifted her hands and Rae and Jennifer watched as white hot flames covered her entire body, shrieking and dancing as they shot up into the sky.

Jennifer's face paled and she took a step back. Even amidst all her bluster, she seemed to sense that this was the end. And although Rae had never seen her run from a fight, her fearless ex-Botcher took off through the parking lot, sprinting like her life depended on it. She had almost reached the other side when a wall of fire sprang up suddenly in front of her and she jumped back. The wall shifted and moved, driving her forward to where Beth was waiting for her.

"I thought this was what you wanted Jenn," she said quietly. "Just you and me."

Jennifer's eyes narrowed and she stepped forward of her own accord. "If I go down, you're going down with me." In a flash, she grabbed a nearby car and literally threw it into the air, sending it hurtling through the sky towards Beth.

Time seemed to slow and Rae reacted on instinct. As Beth lifted her hands protectively in front of her, inadvertently setting the car on fire, Rae leapt into the space in between them, somersaulting mid-air and kicking it back down the other way.

Jennifer screamed as the twisted, molten piece of metal came crashing down upon her. For a split second, Rae saw the look on her face as she watched it fall. But then there was a sickening crash as the car exploded on the pavement, burying Jennifer beneath it in a pile of ash and flames.

"Rae!"

Rae struggled to pull her attention away from the burning car as her mother ran towards her across the lot. "Sweetheart, are you all right?!" She gathered Rae up in her arms, paling in terror as Rae flinched and pulled away.

"I'm fine, I'm fine," she assured her mother, popping her shoulder back into place. "I have a healing tatù, it just takes a minute. What about you?" She looked Beth up and down with sudden concern. "You lost a lot of blood, are you okay?"

Beth shook her hand dismissively. "I've been through worse." Her eyes fell on the burning pile of rubble.

Rae followed her gaze. "I just can't believe it was Jennifer this whole time." She inhaled and cringed as the thick smoke smell filled the air. "All those moments she was alone with me."

Beth shuddered in belated rage. "All those moments I should have been there to protect you."

"Mom, I'm fine," Rae said again, deliberately now avoiding looking at the fire. "It would take more than a little car tossing to do me in." She laughed weakly, but the next second, she felt herself collapsing into a pair of strong arms.

Perfect timing as ever.

"We need to stop meeting like this," Devon murmured into her hair. Rae looked up to answer him, but before she could, his lips were pressed against hers. Ignoring the pain, she wrapped her arms around his neck—pulling herself up higher as the kiss deepened and warmed.

Before she'd nearly had enough, a pointed cough made Devon pull away with a smile.

"Sorry Mrs. Kerrigan," he grinned, stroking the side of Rae's face, "couldn't help myself."

Much to Rae's surprise, her mother walked forward and fondly ruffled his hair. "I quite understand. And Devon? Call me Beth."

Devon's dimple flashed as he beamed back at her. "Beth it is, Mrs. Kerrigan." His eyes trailed over the scorched parking lot. "So does anybody want to tell me what happened here? I came out just as I heard a car explode."

"They said we'd missed the complimentary breakfast," Rae joked before settling herself back in his arms. She still wasn't completely healed and definitely wasn't up for a full interrogation.

"It was Jennifer," Beth explained quickly. "Jennifer was the one who set the fire all those years ago, and it was Jennifer who attacked Luke to steal my files."

Devon's mouth fell open in disbelief. "You've got to be kidding me!" He glanced at the soot-covered, bloody faces of the girls and came round quickly. "That's unbelievable. But that's actually what I was coming over here to tell you." He looked down at Rae with a smile. "Luke's awake. He came out of it about ten minutes ago and now the doctors have him resting. They say he's going to be fine."

Rae closed her eyes in overwhelming relief. "That's good to hear. You have no idea." She pulled out of Devon's arms and tried balancing shakily on her own two feet. "Can I see him?"

Devon shook his head. "Probably not the best idea. His family just got here and I think it would cause more questions than he's ready to answer right now."

Rae nodded quickly. "You're probably right. We've got to get back to Guilder anyway."

"Guilder?" Beth and Devon asked at the same time. "Why Guilder?"

"Because Jennifer wasn't working for herself. There was somebody else involved. Somebody pulling the strings." She inhaled a sharp quick breath as the others held their breaths. "And I think I know who it is. You are not going to believe it. I'm not sure I can."

They stopped at the hospital to have Beth's wound checked and then stitched up. Somehow, though the doctor couldn't explain it, the wound had cauterized, as if it had been burned. Nobody said anything and everyone seemed to be looking in a different direction when the doctor asked.

The ride back to Guilder was quiet and uneventful. When they pulled onto the drive that led between the two towers and the walkway bridge with its Oriel windows, Beth leaned forward and looked around in awe. "So this is what it looks like," she murmured, staring out the window at the sweeping grounds. "I hope all the memories come back." She covered her mouth with her hand. "Argyle came here, it was an all-boys school."

"Rae changed all that," Devon said proudly. "They opened the school to girls specifically to let her in." He nudged her with a grin, but Rae was in no mood to smile. She kept her eyes fixed on the road ahead.

When they pulled up in front of the main building, Carter came running out to meet them. Rae had sent a text to meet at Guilder, not at his office at the Privy Council."

"We heard about what happened," he said in a rush. "This whole time it's been Jennifer, I can't believe it!"

"It wasn't Jennifer," Rae said again as she bypassed him and marched straight for the library.

Carter cast her a strange glance, but kept talking as he, Devon, and Beth trailed along after her. "By the time the PC agents got to the hotel, the fire had mostly burned out. But..." he seemed hesitant to tell them the rest. "...there was no body. No sign of Jennifer anywhere."

Devon threw up his hands. "What the hell do you mean there was no sign of her?! She was trapped under a burning car—we all saw it."

Carter shook his head. "She must have gotten away."

Beth folded her arms across her chest. "That is absolutely unacceptable—"

"So she got away. That's no surprise." Rae shrugged as they entered the library and she led them down to a specific row of books. "There's one more person out there trying to kill me. It's nothing new."

Devon, Beth, and Carter looked at her like she was coming unhinged, but she turned to them with fresh determination.

"She's not the mastermind, she's not the one in charge. Neither was my dad, for that matter." Her mind travelled back to the memory, to the moment when the mysterious man and she had locked eyes. "I know who is. I saw him in Jennifer's mind. I know what he looks like, and I *know* I've seen him here before."

She began flipping through pages of books with ridiculous speed and the rest of her entourage shot each other worried looks.

"Rae," Devon said softly, "this is the historical section. Everything here is at least a hundred years old—"

"Found it!" Rae cut him off with a sudden smile.

She slammed a book down triumphantly on the table and ignored it as the librarian hissed at them to be quiet. The page she'd opened to was an unlabeled sketch, hand drawn and a bit fuzzy, but there was no denying it was the man from Jennifer's memory. The man who'd set this whole thing into motion.

"That's him," she said with certainty. "That's the man behind everything."

Devon stared at the page with a blank expression, but Beth and Carter shot each other an inexplicable stare.

"That's...not possible," Carter murmured.

"Why?" Rae asked impatiently. "Who is he?"

Beth paused a moment, staring at the page, before she turned to face her daughter.

Carter looked at Beth, then slowly to Devon, before finally settling on Rae. He swallowed hard. "That's Jonathon Cromfield."

~ THE END ~
The End in Sight - Coming December 2015

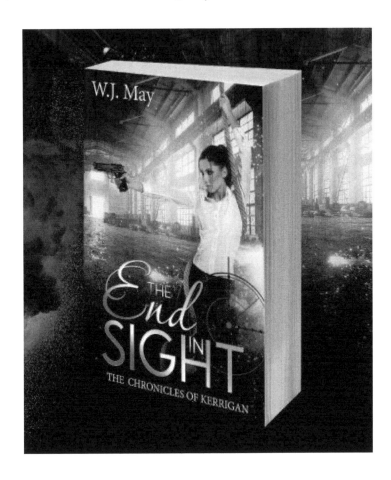

Note from Author;

I hope you enjoyed UNDER FIRE. If you have a moment to post a review to let others know about the story, I'd greatly appreciate it!

I love hearing from my fans so feel free to send me a message on Facebook or by email so we can chat!

I am already working on End in Sight and have high hopes to continue the series after. I'm in no way ready to give up Rae's story. I feel like we are just starting to scratch the surface!

All the best, W.J. May

Newsletter: http://eepurl.com/97aYf

Website: http://www.wanitamay.yolasite.com

Facebook: https://www.facebook.com/pages/Author-WJ-May-FAN-PAGE/141170442608149

The Chronicles of Kerrigan
Book I - *Rae of Hope* **is FREE!**
Book Trailer: http://www.youtube.com/watch?v=gILAwXxx8MU
Book II - *Dark Nebula* **is Now Available**
Book Trailer: http://www.youtube.com/watch?v=Ca24STi_bFM
Book III - *House of Cards* **is Now Available**
Book IV - *Royal Tea* **- Now Available**
Book V - *Under Fire* **– Now Available**
Book VI - *End in Sight,* Coming Fall/Winter 2015

More books by W.J. May

Hidden Secrets Saga:
Download Seventh Mark part 1 For FREE
Book Trailer:
http://www.youtube.com/watch?v=Y-_vVYC1gvo

Book Blurb:

Like most teenagers, Rouge is trying to figure out who she is and what she wants to be. With little knowledge about her past, she has questions but has never tried to find the answers. Everything changes when she befriends a strangely intoxicating family. Siblings Grace and Michael, appear to have secrets which seem connected to Rouge. Her hunch is confirmed when a horrible incident occurs at an outdoor party. Rouge may be the only one who can find the answer.

An ancient journal, a Sioghra necklace and a special mark force life-altering decisions for a girl who grew up unprepared to fight for her life or others.

All secrets have a cost and Rouge's determination to find the truth can only lead to trouble...or something even more sinister.

RADIUM HALOS - THE SENSELESS SERIES
Book 1 is FREE:

Book Blurb:

Everyone needs to be a hero at one point in their life.

The small town of Elliot Lake will never be the same again.

Caught in a sudden thunderstorm, Zoe, a high school senior from Elliot Lake, and five of her friends take shelter in an abandoned uranium mine. Over the next few days, Zoe's hearing sharpens drastically, beyond what any normal human being can detect. She tells her friends, only to learn that four others have an increased sense as well. Only Kieran, the new boy from Scotland, isn't affected.

Fashioning themselves into superheroes, the group tries to stop the strange occurrences happening in their little town. Muggings, break-ins, disappearances, and murder begin to hit too close to home. It leads the team to think someone knows about their secret - someone who wants them all dead.

An incredulous group of heroes. A traitor in the midst. Some dreams are written in blood.

Shadow of Doubt
Part 1 is FREE!
Book Trailer:
http://www.youtube.com/watch?v=LZK09Fe7kgA

Book Blurb:

What happens when you fall for the one you are forbidden to love?

Erebus is a bit of a lost soul. He's a guy so he should be out to have fun but unlike the rest of his kind, he is solemn and withdrawn. That is, until he meets Aurora, a law student at Cornell University. His entire world is shaken. Feelings he's never had and urges he's never understood take over. These strange longings drive him to question everything about himself

When a jealous ex stalks back into his life, he must decide if he is willing to risk everything to be with Aurora. His desire for her could destroy her, or worse, erase his own existence forever.

Courage Runs Red
The Blood Red Series
Book 1 is FREE

Book Blurb:

What if courage was your only option?

When Kallie lands a college interview with the city's new hot-shot police officer, she has no idea everything in her life is about to change. The detective is young, handsome and seems to have an unnatural ability to stop the increasing local crime rate. Detective Liam's particular interest in Kallie sends her heart and head stumbling over each other.

When a raging blood feud between vampires spills into her home, Kallie gets caught in the middle. Torn between love and family loyalty she must find the courage to fight what she fears the most and possibly risk everything, even if it means dying for those she loves.

Free Books:

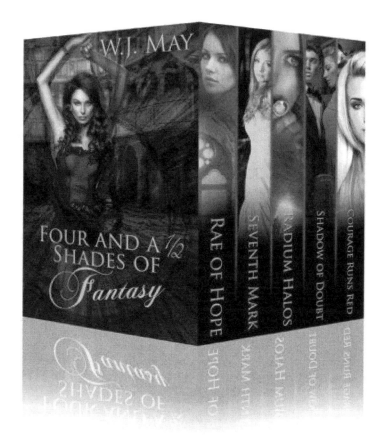

Four and a Half Shades of Fantasy

TUDOR COMPARISON:

Aumbry House——A recess to hold sacred vessels, often found in castle chapels.

Aumbry House was considered very special to hold the female students - their sacred vessels (especially Rae Kerrigan).

Joist House——A timber stretched from wall-to-wall to support floorboards.

Joist House was considered a building of support where the male students could support and help each other.

Oratory——A private chapel in a house.

Private education room in the school where the students were able to practice their gifting and improve their skills. Also used as a banquet - dance hall when needed.

Oriel——A projecting window in a wall; originally a form of porch, often of wood. The original bay windows of the Tudor period. Guilder College majority of windows were oriel.

Rae often felt her life was being watching through one of these windows. Hence the constant reference to them.

Refectory——A communal dining hall. Same termed used in Tudor times.

Scriptorium——A Medieval writing room in which scrolls were also housed.

Used for English classes and still store some of the older books from the Tudor reign (regarding tatùs).

Privy Council——Secret council and "arm of the government" similar to the CIA, etc... In Tudor times, the Privy Council was King Henry's board of advisors and helped run the country.

W.J. May

Did you love *Under Fire*? Then you should read *Four and a Half Shades of Fantasy* by W.J. May!

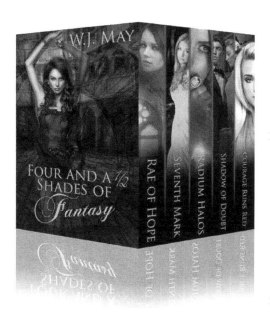

Four (and a half) Fantasy/Romance first Books from five different series! From best-selling author, W.J. May comes an anthology of five great fantasy, paranormal and romance stories. Books included: Rae of Hope from The Chronicles of Kerrigan Seventh Mark - Part 1 from the Hidden Secrets Saga Shadow of Doubt - Part 1 Radium Halos from the Senseless Series and an excerpt from Courage Runs Red from the Red Blood Series

Also by W.J. May

Blood Red Series
Courage Runs Red
The Night Watch

Daughters of Darkness: Victoria's Journey
Victoria

Hidden Secrets Saga
Seventh Mark - Part 1
Seventh Mark - Part 2
Marked By Destiny
Compelled

The Chronicles of Kerrigan
Rae of Hope
Dark Nebula
House of Cards
Royal Tea
Under Fire

The Hidden Secrets Saga
Seventh Mark (part 1 & 2)

The Senseless Series
Radium Halos
Radium Halos - Part 2

Standalone
Shadow of Doubt (Part 1 & 2)
Five Shades of Fantasy

Glow - A Young Adult Fantasy Sampler
Shadow of Doubt - Part 1
Shadow of Doubt - Part 2
Four and a Half Shades of Fantasy
Full Moon
Dream Fighter
What Creeps in the Night
Forest of the Forbidden
HuNted
Arcane Forest: A Fantasy Anthology
Ancient Blood of the Vampire and Werewolf

Made in the USA
Middletown, DE
19 March 2016